THE MAN FROM YESTERDAY

OTHER FIVE STAR WESTERNS BY WAYNE D. OVERHOLSER:

THE MAN FROM YESTERDAY

A WESTERN STORY

WAYNE D. OVERHOLSER

FIVE STAR

A part of Gale, Cengage Learning

GALE
CENGAGE Learning™

Detroit • New York • San Francisco • New Haven, Conn • Waterville, Maine • London

GALE
CENGAGE Learning‑

LIBRARY OF CONGRESS CATALOGING-IN-PUBLICATION DATA

Overholser, Wayne D., 1906–1996.
   The man from yesterday : a Western story / by Wayne D. Over-
holser. — 1st ed.
     p. cm.
   ISBN-13: 978-1-4328-2515-7 (hardcover)
   ISBN-10: 1-4328-2515-1 (hardcover)
   I. Title.
PS3529.V33M36 2010
813'.54—dc22   2010034767

First Edition. First Printing: December 2010.
Published in 2010 in conjunction with Golden West Literary Agency.

Printed in the United States of America
1 2 3 4 5 6 7 14 13 12 11 10

THE MAN FROM YESTERDAY

PROLOGUE

Neal Clark rode in to Cascade City shortly before noon, his Winchester in the boot. He would have gone directly to Olly Earl's hardware store if his father hadn't appeared on the porch of Quinn's Mercantile and motioned to him.

Sam Clark created a multitude of conflicting emotions in the hearts of everyone who knew him, including his son. He was a big-chested, square-headed man, a driver, the kind of person who dominated everyone around him. In the twelve years he had lived on the Deschutes, he had built the Circle C into the biggest outfit on the upper river. That was typical of everything he did.

But there was the other side of his father that Neal knew well. He was a dreamer—some said a visionary. From the first day he had come to the upper Deschutes he had prophesied great things for the country: a railroad, sawmills, irrigation projects, and everything that went into these developments. If anyone else had talked that way, folks would have said he was crazy, but no one had the temerity to venture such an opinion of Sam Clark.

As Neal reined his horse toward the Mercantile, he wondered what was in his father's mind now. It would be something big. He was sure of that. Maybe something wild as well as big. Neal, nineteen and a little short of patience, often wished his father would be satisfied to stay at home and run the Circle C, but he knew that was like wishing for the moon.

"What fetches you to town?" Sam asked.

He stood with his big legs spread, hands shoved under his waistband, his elegant white Stetson tipped back on his forehead. The question irritated Neal because if his father didn't stay home where he belonged, he had no right to question his son's going and coming. At least that was the way it struck Neal, but he didn't let his irritation show. No one did with Sam Clark.

Neal patted the stock of his Winchester. "I want Olly to take a look at my rifle." He jerked his head in the direction of Olly Earl's hardware store. "I missed an easy shot at a buck this morning. Must be something wrong with the sights."

Sam nodded as if he considered that a pretty piddling excuse for riding into town when he should be working. "I'm glad I saw you. Save me a ride to the ranch. I'm going to Prineville this afternoon and I don't know when I'll be home." He stepped off the porch and walked to the hitch rail. "Neal, I'm going to run for the legislature this fall. I've been thinking about it for quite a while. You can manage, can't you?"

Neal nodded, refusing to let his feelings show in his face. This was typical of his father, always seeking something he didn't have when he already had more than enough to make most men satisfied. Actually this new activity wouldn't make much difference regardless of what it entailed because Neal had been rodding the Circle C for more than a year.

"Good luck," Neal said. "I guess you know what you're doing."

"I won't have any trouble being elected," Sam said, his tone briskly confident. "I'll see you in a few days."

He turned and walked back into the Mercantile. Neal rode on down the street to the hardware store. Funny thing about his father who was always working on some project of community betterment, always trying to help someone, yet there was a question in Neal's mind whether his father honestly wanted to give help as much as he wanted to advance his own career. Neal was ashamed of the thought, but he had grounds for thinking it. One thing was sure. Sam Clark was the best-known man on the upper river, and he probably would be elected.

Neal dismounted and tied, then pulled the Winchester from the boot and went into the store. Olly Earl wasn't in sight, so Neal laid the rifle on the counter. Three men rode past the hardware store. Neal glanced at them casually, saw they were strangers, and paid no more attention to them.

He rolled a cigarette and smoked it, wondering if the time would ever come when he was entirely free. Sometimes he doubted his strength, not sure he had a will of his own. Well, that was the price he paid for being his father's son. Apparently it never entered Sam Clark's mind that Neal wanted to do anything except rod the Circle C. It actually was the only thing he wanted to do, but the point was he never had an opportunity to make a choice.

He finished the cigarette and, going to the door, flipped the stub into the street. The three strangers had stopped in front of the bank. Two had gone inside; one remained in front with the horses. Neal stared at the horses, wondering why strangers would go directly to the bank. But maybe they weren't strangers. He didn't know everybody along the Deschutes.

He swung back into the store, his mind turning to Jane Carver. He'd been in love with her for a long time, or so it seemed. She was two years younger than he was, too young, maybe, to get married. Or was she? Was he too young? How did a man know about things like that?

He shook his head, his thoughts going sour. Their ages were no problem, but there was a problem and he might as well face it. What would it do to Jane to move to the Circle C and live exactly the way Sam Clark told her to live?

That was the nub of it, all right. Neal would do the work of running the ranch, but the decisions would be his father's, even down to moving a piece of furniture inside the house. That was the way Sam Clark was made. If Neal took Jane out there, they'd have to accept it as long as Sam was alive.

Suddenly impatient, Neal walked into the back room, calling: "Olly!"

Earl came in from the loading platform. He said: "I didn't know you were here, Neal. I was helping unload some barbed wire." Earl took off his gloves, laid them on a nail keg, and threaded his way through the crated machinery and barrels to where Neal stood. He asked: "What'll you have, son?"

Neal stepped back into the store. "I want you to take a look at my Winchester. The sights aren't right. I had a good chance at a buck and missed him clean."

"Hell, you just had a dose of buck fever," Earl said. He walked behind the counter, and, picking up the rifle, put it to his shoulder and sighted down the barrel. "Loaded?"

"Sure it's loaded."

"Well, can't tell nothing without shooting it," Earl said. "Let's sashay down to the river. Isn't this the gun I sold you last spring?"

Neal nodded. "I haven't used it much. I was used to Dad's old. . . ."

A shot sounded from the street. A .45, Neal thought, and remembered the strangers who had been in front of the bank. He jerked the Winchester from Earl's hands and ran into the street as a second shot shattered the noon silence. Two men raced out of the bank carrying partly filled gunny sacks.

Someone across the street yelled: "Hold-up! Hold-up!"

The one with the horses, so slender that he must have been a kid younger than Neal, threw a shot at the man who had yelled. Neal didn't have time to think about what should be done, no time to make a decision or consider that these men were human beings. They weren't as far as Neal was concerned. They were wolves who had probably murdered the banker, Tom Rollinson, and his cashier, young Henry Abel.

Neal threw the Winchester to his shoulder and cut loose. The first man had reached his horse and was lifting a foot to the stirrup when Neal's bullet hit him. He went down in a rolling fall, his horse bucking along the street.

The second man didn't reach his horse. Neal's next shot cut him down as cleanly as if he'd been yanked off his feet by a rope. The third one, the kid, didn't wait to see what happened. He was in the saddle and hightailing out of town by the time Neal had squeezed off his second shot.

Olly Earl appeared beside Neal, a rifle in his hand. Both of them fired at the fleeing bandit, but he got away. He was riding hard, leaning low on his horse's neck, and, as far as Neal could tell, he hadn't been hit.

Earl threw down his gun in disgust. "We missed him clean," he said bitterly, "but, hell, that rifle of yours is shooting all right. We don't need to try it out."

They ran up the street toward the bank as men rushed out of stores and saloons and the livery stable, with Sam Clark in the lead. Doc Santee left his office on the run, his black bag in his hand. Neal and Olly Earl were the first to reach the fallen men. Neal was still carrying his gun. Doc Santee rushed past them into the bank, Sam Clark a step behind.

Earl knelt beside the outlaws. "Dead." He looked up at Neal. "Son, that was shooting. You got this big bastard through the guts and the other one through the heart." Earl rose. "Where's the sheriff?"

"He's at the M Bar," the liveryman said. "Went out first thing this morning. Said he'd be back by noon."

"Drag 'em over there against the wall and set 'em up," Earl

11

said. "I'm going to take their pictures."

Doc Santee and Sam Clark came out of the bank carrying Henry Abel. Sam said: "Tom's dead. Henry's got a slug in the side. Give us a hand, somebody. Pick up that money and take it inside."

Through all of this Neal stood motionlessly, struggling for each breath. He had killed two men. His mind gripped that fact but could go no further. He stared at the dead men as they were carried to the front wall of the bank and placed against it in a sitting position. Olly Earl returned with his camera and took their pictures, hats off, mouths sagging open, blood oozing from the corners of their lips.

Suddenly Neal was sick. He whirled and ran into a vacant lot next to the bank. There he retched until he was so weak he couldn't stand. Later, he didn't know how much later, Olly Earl came to him and said: "You got no cause to feel bad about what you did. They murdered Tom Rollinson in cold blood and intended to kill Henry. Just bad shooting or they would have."

Neal leaned against the wall, wiping his face with a bandanna. He looked at Earl. "Maybe I got no cause to, Olly, but I never killed a man before. Did you?"

"No," Earl admitted. "Chances are I'd feel just like you if I had. Come on, let's go get a drink."

Neal went with him to O'Hara's saloon and had a drink. The bodies had been taken to Santee's back room. Several men, Quinn and O'Hara and others, came to Neal and shook his hand and told him that all three of the outlaws would have got away if he hadn't done some mighty good shooting, but their words didn't make Neal feel any better, even with the whiskey in him.

"Who were they?" Neal asked.

Nobody knew, but Olly Earl said: "The big one's a middle-aged gent, the other one's young. Maybe in his early twenties.

Father and son, I'd guess. The one that got away is probably another son."

The sheriff, Joe Rolfe, rode into town a few minutes later and took a look at the bodies, but he didn't know them. He picked a small posse and started into the high desert after the boy who had escaped. They returned two days later, tired, dirty, and hungry, with Rolfe shaking his head.

"He must have crawled under a juniper and died," Rolfe said. "We didn't find his horse or nothing. We did pick up his trail a time or two on the other side of Horse Ridge, then lost it. The high desert just swallowed him."

But Neal didn't think the boy was dead. He rode to town every day for two weeks, asking Rolfe if he'd learned anything. Finally Rolfe was able to identify the outlaws Neal had killed by sending the pictures to other sheriffs in the state.

"It was the Shelly gang," Rolfe said. "They've been in a lot of trouble in Lane and Douglas Counties. Came from the hills around Yoncalla. The sheriff in Eugene says the old one was Buck Shelly and the young one his oldest boy named Luke. The kid holding the horses was probably a younger son named Ed."

"If Ed isn't dead," Neal said, "he'll be back."

The old sheriff gave Neal a sharp look. "Son, don't fret yourself about it. I don't think he is alive. You or Olly probably plugged him, and he died of his wounds. But, hell, even if he did make it, he won't be back."

Neal rode home, finding no comfort in Joe Rolfe's words. The sheriff was like Olly Earl, coming around the corner of the bank right after the shooting and telling Neal not to feel bad, then admitting he'd never killed a man. Joe Rolfe could talk until he wore his tongue off at the roots, but the fact was he hadn't killed Ed Shelly's father and brother.

That night Sam Clark showed up at the Circle C. He hadn't been home since the hold-up. The first thing he said was: "I'm taking the bank over, Neal. Somebody's got to run it because this community needs a bank, and I'm the only one who can. I've been a stockholder for quite a while, and I know something about the business. Henry Abel's going to make it. He's a smart banker. We won't have any trouble."

Politics and now the bank. Neal turned away, nervous and irritable. He didn't trust himself to speak. He walked to a window and stared at the bare dirt yard. No grass. No flowers. No foofaraw of any kind because Sam wouldn't stand for it. A strange combination, his father. Standing there, he guessed what was coming before Sam got the words said.

"I've been giving a lot of thought to our affairs." Sam Clark crossed the big living room of the ranch house and placed a hand on Neal's shoulder. "You're going to learn the banking business. Henry Abel will teach you. Oh, not right now. I've got to learn it first. You'll be getting married one of these days and bringing Jane out here to live, but ranch life isn't good for a woman. I'll buy a house in town and you can take over the bank. No hurry, mind you. It'll take a little time to find the right man here."

Neal didn't say anything. He'd always done what his father wanted him to. He had no power to resist. No one did. Sam Clark was like a steam roller. If you argued or resisted, he simply overpowered you and flattened you out and went right on. Now Sam walked away, the idea never occurring to him that Neal might object to having his life managed for him, or that he might prefer running a ranch instead of a bank.

But his father was wrong on one thing, Neal thought. There would be no marriage for a while, not until he knew for sure what had happened to Ed Shelly.

The days passed and no word of any kind came, and when Neal kept asking the sheriff, the old man lost his temper.

"Damn it, can't you forget that ornery devil?" Rolfe said. "I tell you he's dead."

So Neal rode home, his troubled mind finding no comfort. A week later he received a letter postmarked Salt Lake City. The address and letter were printed in pencil and so was the letter.

Someday I'll be back and settle up with you for killing my father and brother.

Ed Shelly

Neal stared at the sheet of paper for a long time, not really surprised, for it was about what he had expected. He had never believed young Shelly was dead. He took the note to Joe Rolfe who shook his head in disgust.

"Some crank," said the sheriff. "Hell, boy, people all over the country read about the hold-up and the killing. For God's sake, Neal . . . forget it. You'll never see or hear of Ed Shelly again."

Neal rode home, jumpy and nervous and wondering if Ed Shelly was hiding behind each pine or lava outcropping that he passed. Maybe Rolfe was right, but that didn't help. Nothing would help, Neal thought, until he knew for sure that Ed Shelly was dead.

CHAPTER ONE

Neal woke at dawn on a chill April morning, trembling and weak and wet with sweat. He'd had the nightmare again. He wondered how many times he'd had it since he'd shot Buck Shelly and his son Luke eight years ago. But the nightmares hadn't started right after the killings. He remembered now. That warning note he'd received from Ed Shelly. The first nightmare. The night after he'd had the note. Yes, that was it. He couldn't forget.

Slowly the trembling passed. He turned his head to look at his wife Jane. She was beautiful. Even in the thin gray light she was beautiful, although he could not see her features distinctly. She was beautiful because he loved her, he guessed. It was equally true with his five-year-old daughter Laurie.

He could not imagine living without Jane and Laurie. That was why the nightmare lingered in his mind with frightening sharpness. It was never quite the same, yet there was always one element that did not vary. Sometimes he arrived home to find that Jane had been murdered. Or that Laurie had been kidnapped. Or he was shot in the back as he walked into the house.

But there was always this faceless man who had done these things. Neal was never able to catch him. He couldn't even describe him because he was invariably a shadowy figure Neal had not seen distinctly, but the knowledge was always in Neal that the man was Ed Shelly. He never discovered how he knew, but he never doubted that he did know.

Now, as always, a restlessness followed the nightmare. Neal couldn't stay in bed, so he eased out from under the covers carefully, hoping he wouldn't waken Jane. He picked up his clothes and slipped out of the room into the hall. He dressed quickly, then glanced into Laurie's room just to be sure she was all right, and, closing the door, went downstairs.

He built a fire in the kitchen range, put the coffee pot on the front, and stepped outside to cut the day's supply of wood. The sun was beginning to show over the juniper-covered ridge to the east, but the air was sharp and he had to work fast to keep warm. That was the only way to retain his sanity. If he was active, he was able to put the nightmare out of his mind.

When he returned to the house, the coffee was ready. He poured a cup, thinking of his father as he stood by the stove waiting for the coffee to cool. Sam Clark had been dead for four years, but he continued to dominate Neal's life. His father had built this house for him and Jane here in Cascade City, and Neal had gone to work in the bank. He often thanked the Lord for Henry Abel. Without him, it was hard to tell what would have happened to the bank.

The hard truth was that Neal's first love was the Circle C. He had often thought of turning the bank over to Abel and taking Jane and Laurie back to the ranch. He wasn't entirely sure why he hadn't unless it was that his father had wanted him to be a banker. But that was only part of the answer. Perhaps it wasn't even a part.

Neal had never been able to talk to anyone about it. Not Jane. Or Joe Rolfe who was still sheriff. Or Doc Santee. He found it hard even to bring it out into the open in his own thinking, but he knew vaguely that it had to do with Ed Shelly, who would someday return to Cascade City. The outlaw would strike at the bank just as his father and brother had done eight years ago. When he did, Neal had to be there.

Jane came in from the dining room just as Neal finished his coffee. She asked anxiously: "Neal, what's the matter this time?"

"Nothing," he said. "I just couldn't sleep."

She came to him and put her arms around him. "You're worried about Ben Darley and Tuck Shelton, aren't you? You've done all you could, darling. You can't go on carrying everybody's troubles on your back."

"I know." He never told her about his nightmares. He always said, as he had just now, that he couldn't sleep. It was crazy, and it would sound even crazier if he told her about it, so he kept it locked up inside him. "Jane, you know how I used to get sore at Dad because he had to run my life like he did everybody else's, but he was a smart man. Now that he's gone, I keep remembering things he told me."

She smiled briefly. "He was a smart man, all right, but I'm not sure he had a heart."

"I think he did," Neal said thoughtfully. "I just remembered this morning how often he said that most folks didn't have any sense about money. They'd save and then turn around and blow it on some fool deal because they were promised big returns. That's exactly what happened here."

She turned away from him, shaking her head, and started getting breakfast. He knew how she felt. Let everybody go ahead and invest their money in Darley's and Shelton's phony irrigation project. It was their business. But Neal couldn't let them do it if he could keep them from it. This was something his father had taught him. It was proof that Sam Clark, for all his arrogant and domineering ways, did have a heart.

They'll hate you, Sam used to say, *but you're smarter than they are, or you wouldn't be where you are. They'll cuss you, sure, but, if you let them throw their money down a rat hole, they'll cuss you for that, too.*

19

Neither Neal nor Jane felt like talking during breakfast. But when he was ready to go, Jane kissed him, and whispered: "Don't let them upset you today, Neal. Please! Laurie and I should come first in your life."

"You do, honey," he said, "but that isn't the point. A man has to do what he has to do, even when he'd rather do something else."

"That's more of what your father taught you," she said with a hint of bitterness. "Many times I've wished he'd been just an ordinary little man like everybody else."

"But he wasn't," Neal said, "and I'm his son. Maybe his shoes don't fit me, but I've got to try to wear them."

He kissed her again and, putting on his hat, left the house. Laurie was still asleep, as she usually was when he left. He walked briskly along the street to the river. There he stopped for a moment, eyes on the water that moved slowly here, very clear and cold. A short distance north of town, it began its swift, tumbling descent to the Columbia. Fog lifted above the water like smoke. It would be gone when the sun rose a little higher. Life was like that, he thought, shifting and vague and transient.

Turning, he strode rapidly up the slope through the pines toward Main Street, his feet silent on the thick bed of long needles. When he reached the corner and turned toward the bank, the thought struck him that there had been little change in the town since his father had died. The railroad, the sawmills, the irrigation projects—still dreams, but Neal had no doubt that in time they would become reality.

For an active, ambitious man, Sam Clark had possessed a great store of patience. Even as a member of the legislature, he had been unable to bring progress to the upper-Deschutes as he had hoped, but he had never become discouraged. *Destiny moves in her own way and at her own speed, and there isn't much any man can do except get things ready,* Sam used to say. In that regard

Neal knew he lacked a great deal. He was not a patient man as his father had been.

He reached the bank, unlocked the front door, and went in. Henry Abel was already there. He had built a fire and was sitting on his high stool near the window, working on a ledger. He liked his job, and he would have been lost without it, but Neal was never quite sure whether he worked long hours because he loved the work, or because the bank was a refuge from his nagging, gossipy wife.

"Good morning, Henry," Neal said as he walked past the teller's cage to his private office. "You're here early."

" 'Morning, Neal," Abel said. "You're early, too."

"I couldn't sleep last night, so I got up." Neal took off his hat and opened the door to his office, then he glanced at Abel, wondering if he ever had nightmares, or if he ever thought about Ed Shelly's return. Abel was under thirty-five, but he looked older, his face pale and pinched. He had not been well since he'd been wounded by the Shellys. He suffered a good deal, especially in cold weather, but Doc Santee said there wasn't anything he could do.

Abel looked up from his ledger. He said: "You're worried, Neal. It won't do any good. It'll take more than worry to stop Ben Darley."

"I aim to use something besides worry," Neal said. "Maybe I'll kill the bastard."

"And hang," Abel said.

Neal went into his office, put his hat on a nail in the wall, and shut the door. That was the trouble, he thought. For the first time in his life, he hated a man enough to kill him, but he didn't hate him enough to hang for it. Beyond any doubt Ben Darley was a crooked promoter, but he had a way of making people trust him. That was simply beyond Neal's understanding. Except for Henry Abel, Joe Rolfe and Doc Santee were the only other men in the county who saw through Darley's scheming.

Neal had several letters to write, but he couldn't get started. He uncorked a bottle of ink, dipped his pen, and wrote *Cascade City, Oregon. April 28.* Then he stopped and leaned back in his swivel chair, his thoughts returning to Ben Darley. The hell of it was Darley had turned old friends against Neal, men like Olly Earl and Mike O'Hara and Harvey Quinn that Neal had known since he'd been a boy.

Neal was still sitting there thinking about it when Abel opened the bank at 9:00 A.M. A moment later he slipped into Neal's office, as silent as a cat in the kangaroo-leather shoes he wore because they were soft and easy on his feet.

"We've got another one," Abel said. "Wants to borrow money to invest with Ben Darley."

"Who is it this time?"

"Jud Manion."

Neal groaned. Of all the men in the county who had asked to borrow money, Manion was the last one he wanted to turn down. During his growing-up years when Sam Clark had been too busy to work at being a father, Jud Manion, riding for the Circle C at the time, took on the job that should have been Sam's.

Manion taught Neal everything he knew about cows and horses and guns and ropes. With infinite patience he had shown Neal how to catch the big ones out of the Deschutes. He had taken the boy hunting. They had even explored the lava caves east of the ranch. Then Manion had fallen in love, and, knowing he couldn't support a family on his $30 a month, he'd taken a homestead. Now this man to whom Neal owed a great debt wanted to borrow money to pour down Ben Darley's crooked rat hole.

As Neal rose and walked to the window, Abel said in his

precise way: "Don't let sentiment blind you, Neal. Not even for Jud."

"How much does he want?"

"One thousand."

"How many have we had this week?"

"Seven."

But Jud Manion was different from the others. At least he was to Neal. He had four children. Six mouths to feed. Six bodies to clothe and keep warm in that tar-paper shack in the junipers. They had existed and that was about all, but now, like almost everyone else in Cascade County, Jud was determined to throw away his means of existence.

"Send him in," Neal said.

Abel hesitated, then he said: "We can't loan him a nickel. His farm's mortgaged now for more than it's worth."

"Send him in."

"He's drunk and he's mean. I can get rid of him. . . ."

"Damn it, send him in!"

Abel slipped out of the office, his thin face showing his disapproval. This wouldn't be easy, Neal knew. Manion seldom got drunk, but, when he did, he was a ring-tailed roarer.

When he came in a moment later and kicked the door shut behind him, Neal saw that Abel was right. Manion was carrying a gun, the first time since he'd left the Circle C as far as Neal knew.

"Glad to see you, Jud." Neal motioned to a chair and, returning to his desk, sat down. "Haven't seen you since I was at your place last month."

Manion didn't sit down. He leaned against the door, scowling at Neal. He was a short, broad-bodied man who worked hard, but he was a poor manager and his farm showed it. He was the only cowboy Neal knew who was trying his hand at farming, and it had gone against his grain from the start.

"I didn't ride in just to pass a few windies," Manion said. "I want to borrow a thousand dollars. Abel says you ain't making no loans these days, but I allowed that didn't mean me."

"It does as far as the bank's concerned," Neal said, "but, if you're up against it, I'll give you my personal check for as much as you need."

"I ain't asking for no hand-out," Manion said. "I've got some security. I own a team, a couple o' milk cows. . . ." He stopped and wiped a hand across his face, anger growing in him. "Damn it, Neal, you know what I've got. You likewise know your bank ain't gonna lose nothing on me."

"What do you want the money for?"

"That ain't none of your business. What does the bank care how I spend money I borrow?"

"It cares a hell of a lot, Jud. Ben Darley and Tuck Shelton are a pair of thieving liars and their irrigation scheme is a swindle from the word go."

Manion stared at Neal with loathing. "You're turning out worse'n Sam. All the time I was trying to teach you something. . . ."

"I know what I owe you, Jud." Neal rose. "I'll do anything I can for you. I said for you, Jud, not Ben Darley and Tuck Shelton."

Manion walked to the desk, so furious he was trembling. "Sam or you have run this bank for years. What have either one of you done for this country? Nothing! Just nothing! Now Darley gives us a chance to make some money and develop the country to boot, but you're so damned ornery you won't let any of us take it."

"I'm trying to keep you from losing what you have got," Neal said patiently. "Maybe you can't see it now. . . ."

Manion interrupted with an oath. "It's like Darley says. You wanted a controlling interest in the deal, but he figured it was smarter to let all of us in on it than to help make a banker fatter'n he is already."

"Darley's a liar," Neal said. "I never offered to put a nickel into his scheme."

"You're the liar," Manion shot back. "Darley's got a letter of your'n saying you wanted to buy fifty thousand dollars' worth of stock."

"Ever see the letter?"

"Alec Tuttle and Vince Sailor have." Manion clenched his big fists. "I never thought you'd go like this, but I was dead wrong. Put a man behind a banker's desk and something happens to him every time."

"I'm sorry you feel that way," Neal said.

Manion didn't leave. He stood there, the corners of his mouth working like a child struggling to hold back the tears. He put a hand on the butt of his gun. "Neal, I've got to have that money. You don't know how it is to have a wife and four kids who never get enough to eat. I work sixteen hours a day, but I can't make enough to feed 'em. Darley says he'll still let me in, if I can get the money. He says every share of stock will double in value in six months."

"It won't, Jud." Neal laid a gold eagle on the desk. "Take it. Buy the grub you need. I'll give you more when that's gone. Or you can get your old job on the Circle C."

"A thousand dollars, Neal." Manion drew his gun. "Give it to me or I'll kill you. I've been shoved a long ways since we used to ride together . . . downhill all the time . . . but you ain't gonna make me lose this chance."

"Put that gun away, you fool."

"I ain't a fool." Manion raised the gun, the hammer back. "You never heard a baby cry all night because he's hungry. I have. My babies, Neal. All I'm asking for is a chance to take care of 'em. Write me a check. Or call Abel in here and have him give me the cash. I don't care how you do it. Just see that I get it."

Hard work and privation and a little whiskey had turned Jud Manion's head. Looking at him now, a big, trembling misfit of a farmer, Neal knew he would do exactly what he said. He'd be sorry about it later, but by then Neal Clark would be a dead man.

"I'll give you ten seconds," Manion whispered. "I can't wait no longer."

"They'll hang you."

"I don't care. Gimme the money so I can take it to Darley before it's too late."

The office door slammed open. Startled, Manion whirled and fired, but Abel had lunged sideways out of range. The instant Manion started to turn, Neal dived, headfirst, over the desk. Manion threw a shot at him, a wild shot that missed by five feet, then he was going back, and down, Neal on top of him.

Manion hit the floor hard, the wind jarred out of him. He struck at Neal, but there was no real power in the blow. Neal twisted the gun out of his hand and rose, breathing hard.

"You've gone crazy, Jud," Neal said. "I ought to turn you over to Joe Rolfe."

"You're crazy if you don't," Abel said. "He'll try it again."

"No, I can't do it, but I'll keep his gun." Neal turned to the desk and, picking up the $20 gold piece, dropped it into Manion's shirt pocket. "Go get that grub for your kids."

Jud rose, looking at Neal with no repentance or regret in his eyes whatever. "Abel's right. Taking my gun won't stop me." He walked out, reeling a little.

Abel said: "You're soft, Neal. Too soft."

Neal shut the door, leaving Abel outside. Maybe he was soft, softer than Sam Clark would have been under the circumstances, but he wasn't his father and he was glad of it. He walked to the window, still breathing hard. He'd been scared, and he had a right to be, with Jud Manion half crazy as he had been.

A wind had come up in the sudden, gusty way that was typical of April, blowing so much dust that he couldn't see the Signal Butte Inn on the other side of the street. Staring moodily into the gray fog, Neal thought that being a banker hadn't been so bad until Ben Darley came to town with his wife Fay and his partner, Tuck Shelton.

They had rented the office rooms over Quinn's Mercantile and started promoting an irrigation project on the high desert east of town. Darley was a smooth operator, the smoothest Neal had ever seen. He'd made big promises of quick profit, so it was natural enough, Neal thought, for the farmers and townspeople to swallow the man's lies.

Neal walked back to his desk, the smoldering hatred he felt for Ben Darley suddenly fanned into flame. He couldn't blame Jud Manion for trying to kill him, but it would never have happened if Darley hadn't come to Cascade City.

One solution was to kill Darley. Neal opened the top drawer of his desk and took out a loaded .38. He remembered his father saying: *A bank occupies a special position in a small community like this. Sometimes it has to protect people from themselves.*

That was exactly what he had tried to do when he'd turned down requests for loans to invest with Darley. But why should he make enemies out of friends who wanted to go broke? It was a good question. Still, he couldn't rid himself of other people's burdens. Jane had told him he couldn't carry all of them on his back, but they were there just the same.

Then, staring at the gun, he made his decision. He'd see Darley. A lot of problems would be solved if he were forced to kill Ben Darley.

He slipped the gun into his pocket, buttoned his coat, and, taking his hat off the nail, left the bank.

CHAPTER TWO

Ben Darley and Tuck Shelton's office was over Harvey Quinn's Mercantile, across the street and at the other end of the block from the bank. Neal paused on the boardwalk, looking at the men who sat on the weathered benches in front of the Signal Butte Inn. Alec Tuttle and Vince Sailor were among them, two farmers who were more vocal than the others in condemning the bank for its attitude toward the Darley-Shelton project. Jud Manion was not with them, and Neal was thankful for that.

Still he hesitated, wondering if this was the day the smoldering trouble would break into flame. He shrugged his shoulders and crossed the street, hoping there would be no trouble with these men who were his neighbors and had been his friends. But friendship was too often a transient thing, and lately he'd a feeling that trouble with these men was inevitable.

The wind was still blowing, although it was not gusty and dust-laden as it had been a few minutes before. Neal tugged at his hat brim, setting it more firmly on his head so the wind wouldn't send it rolling down the street. The last thing he wanted to do was to run after his hat in front of the men who were sitting on the bench of the Signal Butte Inn.

As it was, he felt their eyes on him before he reached the boardwalk. If they jumped him, he'd have a hell of a fight on his hands. Ben Darley was the man he wanted, not Tuttle or Sailor or any of the other farmers who were eyeing him with cold malevolence.

Neal felt the weight of the gun in his pocket, but he couldn't use it on these men, even in self-defense. They hated him, but it was a kind of childish hatred, as if he had deprived them of candy that had been dangled in front of them for weeks.

Neal was directly in front of Tuttle when the man said: "Clark."

Stopping, Neal looked down at the man. He said: "Well?"

He had made a mistake crossing the street here. It had been an act of bravado. He hadn't wanted Tuttle or any of them to think he was afraid. Now he realized he should have kept his mind on Ben Darley and let Tuttle and his friends think what they wanted to.

Tuttle let the seconds ribbon out, then he said: "I hear Jud Manion has joined our club, and him claiming it would be different because he was your friend. I wish to hell he'd have drilled you. We heard the shooting and figured he had."

The time when Neal could have reasoned with them was long past, so he didn't try. He said: "I guess that's the way you would have liked it."

He would have gone on if Vince Sailor hadn't jumped up and grabbed his arm. He was a tall, jaundiced-looking man, so thin that the old saw about having to stand up twice to cast a shadow was used repeatedly to describe him.

Neal jerked free from the claw-like hands as Sailor said: "Maybe we could get a loan from the bank if we wore boots and a ten-gallon hat like you do, but we're farmers, Clark. Is that why your bank won't loan us any money?"

"No, Vince," Neal said. "You know it isn't."

"I ain't so sure, Moneybags," Sailor said contemptuously. "It's too bad for us that the only bank in the county is run by a son-of-a-bitch who thinks nothing is important but cows. Ninety-five percent of the people in this county are farmers. Are you too bull-headed to admit that?"

"No, I'll admit it," Neal said.

This accusation that he was a cowman and was prejudiced against farmers was a fiction that Ben Darley had built up in the minds of all the farmers and most of the townsmen. Sam Clark had been a rancher before he was a banker, and Neal had run the Circle C for years before he had taken the bank over, so he habitually dressed like a rancher because he was more comfortable than he would have been in a sedate business suit such as Henry Abel wore. These were the facts that Darley, skilled operator that he was, had played upon successfully.

Neal knew there wasn't the slightest use to deny anything or explain his position. He had attempted too many times and had not been believed, so he tried to go on, but Tuttle grabbed his arm just as Sailor had a moment before. He was set for trouble and nothing else would satisfy him.

"Listen to me, you bastard," Tuttle said. "You wouldn't lose a nickel loaning us money, but you're so damned afraid that one of us will amount to something in this county you won't. . . ."

Neal jerked free. "You're pushing, Alec. You're pushing too hard."

Tuttle laughed. "I'm just starting to push, mister." And he swung.

Sensing this was coming, Neal ducked Tuttle's wild blow and drove a straight right squarely to the point of the big farmer's chin, knocking him off the walk into the street. Neal jumped back and whirled, expecting the men on the bench to rush him. They would have, he thought, if they hadn't seen Joe Rolfe coming along the walk. So they sat there, sullenly silent except for Sailor who called: "Kill him, Alec! Kill the son-of-a-bitch!"

Tuttle got to his feet and shook himself, cursing. He came at Neal with both fists swinging, a powerful man, but an awkward one. Neal knew how to handle himself, for he had done his share of fighting when he was younger, even taking boxing lessons from a drifter who was riding the grub line but had been a professional in his younger days. Neal cut Tuttle down as efficiently as if he were using an axe on a pine tree, a right and then a left, and Tuttle was on his back again.

"Get up, Alec," Sailor begged. "Get up, damn it. You can't let a man who sits on his rump in a bank all day lick you like that."

Tuttle tried. He struggled to his hands and knees, looking up at Neal, blood running into his mouth from his nose. He licked his upper lip, spit out a mouthful of blood, and lunged forward, big arms spread. The very weight of his charge carried him into Neal. A right to the side of the head didn't stop him. Neal stumbled back, Tuttle's arms around his middle, hugging him as he tried to squeeze breath out of him.

Still retreating, Neal stayed on his feet as he supported almost the entire weight of the big man. For a moment he was afraid he was going down. If Tuttle got him into the dust of the street, it would be a different fight, Tuttle's kind of fight. Neal had seen him whip too many men to want any part of it. He hit Tuttle on one side of the head and then the other, but still the heavy arms hugged him, Tuttle's head shoving hard against his stomach.

The man was like a grizzly. Now the pressure was beginning to take its toll. Neal couldn't breathe. Red devils danced in front of his eyes. In desperation, he brought his right fist down squarely on the back of Tuttle's thick neck, a blow that might have killed a lesser man.

Tuttle's grip went slack. Neal stepped back and let the man fall face down into the dust. He lay motionlessly. Neal looked at the men on the bench; he heard Vince Sailor's bitter cursing, then he turned to Joe Rolfe.

He said: "I hope he broke his damned neck. You holding me, Joe?"

Rolfe knelt beside Tuttle and turned him over. He stood up,

his face gray as he shook his head at Neal. "Not this time," he said. "Go on before somebody else tries to whip you."

Neal swung around and strode on to the Mercantile, more thoroughly convinced than ever that only Ben Darley's death could bring peace back to the Deschutes.

CHAPTER THREE

Neal's face showed no marks, but his ribs hurt from the pressure Tuttle had applied to his sides. The thought occurred to him that Darley might have put Tuttle and Sailor up to starting the fight. Darley claimed he needed only a few more thousand dollars to start work, and he blamed Neal because the money had not been raised. If Neal were killed in a street brawl, Darley would be free of his principal opponent without raising a hand.

At the foot of the stairs that led to the office rooms over the Mercantile Neal met Tuck Shelton. He paused, not sure whether this was trouble or not. After Jud Manion had pulled a gun on him and Tuttle had started a fight, he could expect anything.

Shelton stopped, his pale blue eyes on Neal. He was a strange man, silent and withdrawn. He was average-looking, average-size, the kind of man who never seemed to warrant a second glance. He was younger than Darley by a good ten years. When he did speak, which was seldom, his voice was soft and inoffensive. From the first Neal had wondered how Shelton fitted into the irrigation scheme, for Darley had done all the work.

"Looking for me?" Shelton asked, smiling as if he had some secret knowledge that was not known to Neal.

"No," Neal answered. "I want to see Darley."

"He's in the office," Shelton said, and went on.

Neal stared after him, thinking that Darley claimed his partner was the real brains of the company, but Joe Rolfe, who was a good judge of men, had another idea. "Watch out for

34

Shelton," Rolfe had said. "He's hiding behind that easy way of his. He's got the eyes of a killer. I'm guessing that's what he's here for, if Darley needs any killing done."

Neal had been surprised at that, then suddenly it struck him that he had never actually noticed the man's eyes. After that he had. They were strange eyes, with too much white like the eyes of an outlaw horse. At times Neal had surprised him by staring at him, his face had turned bitter.

But now as Neal climbed the stairs, he realized he had never learned anything from Shelton's expressions. Usually they held as little feeling as if they were made of glass. He put the man out of his mind. Darley, not Shelton, was responsible for what had been happening in Cascade County.

Neal's quarrel was not with Jud Manion or Tuttle or Sailor. They had simply been carried away by Darley's glowing promises. If he could show them what the man was, their attitude would change. But how could you prove anything to people whose minds were closed?

At this moment Neal did not have the slightest idea how to answer that question, and he doubted his own good sense in coming here. Darley was too slick to attempt to use a gun. No matter how much Neal wanted to kill him, he knew he was incapable of killing any man who refused to fight.

Well, he'd come too far to back out. He paused in the hall, staring at the black letters on the glass half of the door: *DARLEY AND SHELTON DEVELOPMENT COMPANY.* It looked solid and dependable, just as the brochures did that had been spread all over central Oregon with pictures of Darley and the lakes he intended to tap for irrigation. The writing was dignified, never flamboyant. The final perfect touch was the blackface type at the bottom of each page: *WE ARE HERE TO STAY.*

Smart! Plenty smart. You had to say that for them. Shelton might be the brains, or he might be the gunslinger, but there

35

was no doubt about Darley. He was the front, the contact man, the one who did the talking and made all the public appearances and shook hands; he was the substance, Shelton the shadow.

Not once as far as Neal knew had Darley ever made a definite, get-rich-quick promise that could be pinned down as to time and place or percentage of profit. Still, he had consistently inferred that those who invested in his company would soon double their money. Therein lay the man's skill.

Darley had the appearance of an honest, humble man, the kind people instinctively trusted. He talked glibly about what his project would do for the county and the town, bringing life to a parched desert, creating homes for hundreds of families, making possible the raising of more food for a rapidly expanding nation that was wearing out its best soil. Then he would recite figures about the profits earned by other irrigation projects, invariably picking the most successful ones and overlooking those that had failed.

When he made a speech, Darley always finished with the statement that he and Tuck Shelton were bringing $50,000 of their own money to the project. If the people of the community had faith in central Oregon, they'd raise another $50,000. Work would start on the project the day the company had $100,000 in the treasury, for that was the amount it would take to complete the ditch. He would not, he said, turn a shovelful of dirt until he could assure both the investors and prospective settlers that the project could be successfully completed.

Neal did not believe Darley and Shelton had $50,000 of their own, and he was convinced that more than $50,000 in stock had been sold.

He opened the door and went in, feeling the weight of the gun in his pocket. Now that he was here, having been prompted by a cold-blooded desire to kill a man, he wished he had left the gun in the bank. If Darley did force a fight and Neal killed him, the men outside would never believe it was anything but murder.

He closed the door, glancing around the room. This was the reception room, furnished with several rawhide-bottom chairs, a hat rack, and a desk where Mrs. Darley worked. She served as receptionist and bookkeeper, working for nothing, Darley told the stockholders, because she believed in what the company was doing and wanted to do her part.

Neal would have turned around and left, thinking to hell with it, if Mrs. Darley had not glanced up from a ledger, and rose, a smiling, handsome woman in her early thirties.

Now pride would not let Neal go. He stood there while Mrs. Darley moved toward him, her hips swaying a little but not too much, just enough to touch a torch to a man's imagination without promising anything. Neal had talked to her a few times, and on each occasion she had bothered him because he sensed she was an eager, vibrant woman with keen animal desire.

As he watched her, he was possessed again by the haunting hunger he felt every time he was with her. He was instantly ashamed, for he was completely in love with Jane, who was everything a man could want in a wife.

She held out her hand, and, when he took it, she let it remain longer than necessary in his, asking: "What brings the enemy here?"

"I want to see your husband," he said.

She stood looking at him, her face quite close to his, her full, red lips slightly parted at the center. Her eyes were dark brown, her hair so black that it seemed to hold a blue tone. She was wearing a brown skirt and white shirtwaist that was buttoned sedately under the chin, a manner of dress that marked her as a very moral and respectable person.

Just as Ben Darley managed to convey the impression he was honest and idealistic, so his wife kept within the bounds of propriety in both her manner of dressing and her behavior. Still, she contrived to let Neal know the respectable-appearing woman was not the real Fay Darley.

"I have a great admiration for you, Mister Clark," she said. "Everybody in town says you're wrong about us, but that doesn't change you. You're the kind who would go after anything you wanted, wouldn't you?"

"I guess I would," he said.

"I'll tell Ben you're here." She started toward the door of Darley's private office, then stopped and turned her head to look at Neal. "If you went after something you really wanted, I believe you'd get it."

He liked the way she held her shoulders; he watched the sweep of her firm, perfectly pointed breasts. With an effort he turned to look at the big map on the wall of the proposed project, his throat suddenly dry. He heard her laugh as she went on into Darley's office, as if she sensed the effect she had upon him and was pleased.

She was gone for several minutes. Neal could hear the hum of talk, but he could not make out the words. He stood there, studying the wall map that showed the Deschutes River, Cascade City, and the Barney Mountain area with the two lakes near the summit. The lakes, he saw, were drawn far larger in proportion to the country around them than they actually were. From the eastern edge of Big Lake a dotted line representing the proposed ditch curled down the slope in a northerly direction.

Beyond the end of the line was the high desert with its tens of thousands of acres of Public Domain waiting to be taken by land-hungry settlers. Water was the only thing that was needed, Darley had said repeatedly. Like many lies that are spoken often enough, it had finally been accepted.

For years Neal had run cattle on the high desert. He knew

there were two other factors Darley ignored that would whip the project regardless of the water supply. One was the short growing season. It was short enough here on the Deschutes, but not nearly as short as it was on the high desert.

The second, and this was the one that proved to Neal that Darley was a liar and a crook, was the fact that the ditch had to be built across miles of lava rock, not through dirt that would be comparatively inexpensive to move. The water would have to be carried by wooden or steel flumes because blasting the lava would open up seams through which the water would trickle away.

Neal knew $100,000 would not begin to pay for the miles of flume that would be necessary, a point Darley generally managed to evade. Once, when he had been pinned down in a public meeting, he had answered that he had the right business connections. He could buy metal fluming, he said, for a fraction of what it had cost the companies that had developed the projects along the river, a statement Neal knew was a lie.

Fay Darley opened the door and walked toward Neal. "I'm sorry I kept you waiting, Mister Clark, but I'm leaving now and there were a few things I had to talk to Ben about." She put her hands on his arms and pulled him toward her. He felt the pressure of her breasts, he smelled her perfume, and he heard her whisper—her lips were close to his ear—"Be careful. Be awfully careful." Then she hurried out of the office.

Neal stood rooted there, thoroughly disturbed by what she had just done. He brushed a hand across his face and looked at the sweat on his fingertips, then wiped his hands on his coat, convinced she was a wanton and startled because, knowing what she was, she still affected him the way she did.

He walked into Darley's private office and stopped, flat-footed.

The promoter was standing behind his desk, a cocked gun

lined on Neal's chest. He said: "I can think of only one reason for you to come here, Clark. It won't work. I propose to kill you before you have a chance to kill me."

CHAPTER FOUR

For a long moment Neal stood just inside the door of Ben Darley's private office, the sound of his labored breathing a rasping noise in his ears. He was completely dumbfounded, not even suspecting that Darley owned a gun. Tuck Shelton, yes, but not Darley.

Neal had known Darley as a homely, awkward-appearing man, slightly stooped, and plagued by a speech impediment that gave the impression he was pausing often to select the right word for the particular occasion. He appeared to be the exact opposite of the sleek, attractive animal who was his wife, possessing qualities that would have been fatal for many tasks, but were exactly the characteristics he needed to convince people he was humble, honest, and unselfish.

Now, staring across the room at him, Neal saw a different Ben Darley than the stockholders saw when they talked to him about the project. He was homely enough, for nothing could change his rough, irregular features. In every other way he was changed. He was not stooped. He spoke without the slightest difficulty. And there was nothing awkward about the way he held his gun.

For a moment panic gripped Neal. Darley could murder him with reasonable safety. He could claim self-defense and people would believe him, for everyone knew how Neal felt. All Darley needed to do was shoot him, fire the gun in Neal's pocket, drop the gun on the floor, and get Joe Rolfe.

The panic passed as quickly as it had come. Darley, a careful man, wasn't one to take chances. Neal said: "You can't pull it off, Darley. You'll have a little trouble proving it was self-defense to Joe Rolfe."

Darley's indecision held him motionless for a time. He chewed on his upper lip, then he said: "Why did you come here, Clark?"

"I'd like to kill you, Darley," Neal said. "Don't make any mistake about that, but I'll never get you into the street for a fair fight."

"Shelton will oblige you," Darley said.

"It's got to be you," Neal said. "Shelton may be the brains of your outfit, but you're the man people believe in."

It was a left-handed kind of compliment, and Darley seemed amused. "I'll ask you again. Why are you here?"

"I wanted to talk," Neal said, aware that there was nothing he could do but play for time and hope to leave here alive.

"Talk," the promoter said hotly. "Well, mister, I've had too damned much of your talk already. You've done everything you could to block us from the day we moved in here."

"And I've just heard too much of your talk," Neal shot back. "The second-hand kind. Jud Manion told me Tuttle and Sailor claim they've seen a letter from me asking to buy fifty thousand dollars' worth of your stock. Somebody's lying and I figure it's you."

To Neal's surprise Darley laid the gun on his desk and sat down. He motioned to a chair. "Sit down, Clark. We'll talk, but I don't know what good it'll do you. Sure I lied. I forged your name to a letter for Tuttle and Sailor to see. They gave you a cussing, mister, a hell of a good cussing."

Neal dropped into the chair across the desk from Darley. He said: "I'll say one thing for you, Darley, you're a good actor. You'd have to be to convince people you're a saint when actually you're a liar and a thief."

Darley's thick lips thinned in a grin. "Now I'll tell you what I think of you. You're stupid, Clark, too stupid to run a bank. If you made the loans folks want, and if you're right about me, you could take over every farm in the county."

"Maybe a stupid man sleeps better than a crook." Neal leaned forward. "How much would it take to get you and Shelton to return the money you've taken in and leave the county?"

"More than you've got." Darley laughed. "You're wasting your time. You don't have an ace in your hand. People don't like you, and, before this is over, they'll hang you."

"They'll hang you first," Neal said, "because you're wrong about me not having an ace. The figures you've been quoting for construction of a ditch are phony. I've got a survey crew working out there now. They'll be finished in a day or two, and then I'll have the information I need to prove you're a crook."

For a moment Darley's surprise shattered his composure, then the mask was in place again. "You're bluffing. News like that gets around and I haven't heard it." He rose and moved to the end of the desk, his gun still within easy reach. "I'm busy."

Neal glanced at the big safe in the corner, remembering what a job it had been to pull it up the stairs and get it into place here. At the time he'd wondered why Darley and Shelton needed such a heavy safe, but now he thought he knew. The money that had been collected was right there, not in a Portland bank as Darley claimed.

"What happens if someone cracks that safe and cleans you out?"

"They won't. Shelton sleeps here every night. Don't try it, Clark. It's all the boys would need to string you up."

"When are you starting work on the ditch?"

"When do you think?"

"Never."

Darley's patience suddenly snapped like a frayed rope. "You seem able to answer your own questions. Now get to hell out of here and let me alone."

Still Neal didn't move. He stood with his feet spread, eyes on Darley. He had been afraid when he'd come in and faced a gun in Darley's hand. Darley had been scared and was therefore dangerous, but he'd ceased to be dangerous the moment he'd laid his gun down. Now, thinking about what had been said, fury suddenly boiled up in Neal. With no one to hear, Darley had tacitly admitted that everything Neal suspected was true.

"I've lost almost every friend I had in the county on your account," Neal said, "and that includes Jud Manion. He was in the bank today, talking about hearing his baby cry because he was hungry. If you get away with this, there'll be babies crying all over the county."

"You trying to make me cry like the babies?" Darley motioned toward the door. "Damn it, get out of here before I throw you out."

"Try it," Neal challenged. "You're a bastard, Darley, a stinking, lying, stealing son-of-a-bitch."

One moment Darley was standing there, his hands at his sides. The next he had exploded into action, a fist catching Neal on the chin and sending him reeling. If Darley had followed up, he might have whipped Neal, but the blow seemed to be an expression of his anger and he was satisfied to let it go at that. Neal wasn't. He rushed the promoter, smashing Darley's defensive fists aside and driving home a roundhouse right that knocked Darley flat on his back.

Darley got up and charged back. They stood there for a time exchanging blows, both willing to take one to give one. That was another mistake on Darley's part because he lacked the hatred that had grown in Neal for months. He was a madman, not feeling Darley's fists as he hammered wicked punches to

44

the promoter's face, then his stomach, then the face again. A better man than Darley could not have stood up under that kind of punishment. He backed up, got his feet tangled in a wastebasket, and fell headlong, shaking the floor and rattling the pictures on the wall.

Darley rolled and got to his feet, whimpering like a hurt pup. He lunged toward the desk, shoved the chair back, and, crawling under the desk, rolled up into a ball, his head buried in his arms.

Neal got him by the coat collar and hauled him to his feet. Darley grabbed for the gun on the desk, but didn't quite reach it. Neal hit him again, spinning him back toward a file cabinet. It went over with a tremendous clatter, papers spilling all over the floor, Darley falling across it.

Darley got up and charged Neal again, swinging both fists wildly, but he had been hurt too much for his blows to be effective. Neal ducked and drove at Darley, pumping a right and left into the promoter's middle, then catching him squarely on the jaw with an upswinging right. This time Darley went down and stayed down.

Neal would have hauled Darley to his feet and hit him again if Shelton had not called from the door: "That's enough, Clark!"

Neal straightened, wiping a coat sleeve across his face. Blood was pounding in his head with pulsating throbs. He squeezed his eyes shut and opened them. He could see Shelton clearly then, standing in the doorway, a gun in his hand.

"Don't make a fast move, Clark." Shelton glanced at Darley's battered face and shook his head. "You did quite a job, but don't try it with me, or I'll kill you."

Shelton backed into the front office, motioning for Neal to follow, the gun not wavering from Neal's chest. He seemed completely impersonal about this, but there was no doubt in Neal's mind that Joe Rolfe's estimate of the man was right.

Under ordinary circumstances he was the most colorless man in town, the kind who could be in a crowd and afterward everyone would swear he hadn't been there at all. But right now he was a killing machine.

Shelton moved behind Fay Darley's desk, motioning toward the door that opened into the hall. Neal walked past the big map on the wall to the hat rack near the door, his gaze fixed on Shelton's face. There seemed to be more white in his eyes than ever; he was nervous and jumpy as if fighting a compulsion to kill Neal where he stood.

When Neal reached for his Stetson, Shelton said: "Keep going, friend. Right on out of town. Ben won't forget this. Neither will I."

His face was not ordinary now. It was contorted by a feral bitterness such as Neal had never seen on the face of any man before in his life. He left the office quickly, closing the door behind him, and went down the stairs. He knew he was lucky to be alive, that it would have taken only the slightest wrong move on his part to have made Shelton pull the trigger.

Neal dropped a hand into his coat pocket and felt of the gun. He considered going back and shooting it out with Shelton, but gave up the thought at once, remembering that Shelton's death would change nothing.

His fingers closed over a folded piece of paper. His pocket had been empty when he'd put the gun there earlier in the morning. He drew the paper out and unfolded it. A note had been printed with a dull pencil.

A man never escapes from what he did yesterday. When the time comes, I'll get square with you for what you done to my father and brother.

Ed Shelly

Neal leaned against the wall, staring at the note. For a moment he wondered if he were asleep, if this were part of the nightmare that was so terribly familiar. Then he began to tremble and shoved the note back into his pocket. No, this wasn't a nightmare. He was very much awake, and he had the weird feeling that he had lived through this moment before, a moment he had been sure for eight years would come sooner or later. But coming just now, on top of everything else. . . .

Very slowly he went down the steps, one hand clutching the rail.

CHAPTER FIVE

When Neal reached the boardwalk at the foot of the stairs, he saw that the crowd of men that had been in front of the Signal Butte Inn was gone. No one was in sight except Joe Rolfe, who stood at one end of the horse trough, his hands in his pockets, the afternoon sun reflected in the star he wore on his shirt.

This was the same star Rolfe had worn as long as Neal could remember, and it was as shiny now as it had been years ago when Neal had stared admiringly at it as a child. Rolfe's long term as sheriff was as shiny bright as the star. In Neal's mind he was the only man in Cascade County with the exception of Doc Santee whose honesty and integrity were above suspicion.

"What have you been into now?" Rolfe asked.

"Had a fight with Darley."

Neal handed the sheriff the paper he had found in his pocket and walked on past him to the horse trough.

"You're having a right busy day," Rolfe said, not looking at the paper. "A ruckus with Tuttle and now one with Darley."

"And Jud Manion trying to hold me up for a thousand dollars," Neal said, "and Tuck Shelton throwing his gun on me and running me out of their office. Now that."

Neal sloshed water over his face, and dried with his bandanna. When he looked at Rolfe, the sheriff was staring at the note, as motionless as if he were paralyzed. Two townsmen walked by, both nodding at Rolfe and ignoring Neal. One was Dick Bishop, the jeweler, the other Olly Earl, who owned the hardware store.

48

Neal had known them as long as they'd been in town, but now they passed him as if he were an unwelcome stranger in Cascade City.

Neal watched the two men until they disappeared into O'Hara's bar, but the old smoldering anger that had been in him for weeks since he had been ostracized by both farmers and townsmen did not break into flame as it had so many times. A man had to do what he had to do regardless of petty opposition, and this was hardly even petty after what Neal had been through today.

Still Rolfe stood staring at the note as if he were hypnotized by it. He was nearly seventy, his back as straight as a plumb line, and slender without the slightest hint of a paunch. When it came to trailing a fugitive, he could outride a man twenty years younger. His face, as withered and brown as an apple that had hung on the tree after a hard winter, betrayed no emotion when he folded the paper and slipped it into his coat pocket. He pinned his dark eyes on Neal, right hand coming up to curl a tip of his sweeping white mustache.

"Where'd you get it?" Rolfe asked.

"It was in my coat pocket. I didn't know it was there until after I left Darley's office just now."

"You trying to say somebody shoved it into your pocket without you knowing it?"

"That's exactly what I'm saying."

"Who had a chance to do it?"

"It wasn't there when I left home this morning," Neal said. "Must have happened today. Could have been any of a dozen people. Jud Manion. Henry Abel. Sailor or Tuttle. Missus Darley. Maybe Shelton." He frowned, thinking of Mrs. Darley. She'd had the best opportunity of anyone. She could have dropped a rock into his pocket without him knowing it when she'd stood close to him in her husband's office. "Missus Darley," he said thoughtfully. "Joe, I think she was the one."

Rolfe got his pipe out of his pocket and began to fill it. "Any stranger who comes to this burg is going to hear about that Shelly business," he said thoughtfully. "Folks still like to talk about it. Now if Darley or Shelton could get you to thinking about that and worrying enough, you'd quit fighting them. It makes sense, Neal. It's almost clean-up time for them two bastards, and you've been a burr under their tails right from the first."

"Could be, all right," Neal admitted. "I suppose I might as well forget it. Joe, a while ago Darley practically admitted they have no intention of digging a ditch."

"That ain't news," Rolfe said irritably, "but you didn't prove nothing by going up there and scrapping with Darley."

"I know it. I aimed to kill the son-of-a-bitch if I could get him to go for his gun, but it didn't work that way."

"Lucky for you it didn't," Rolfe said. "If you're figuring to smoke it out with Darley, you'd better have a crowd of witnesses." He held a match to his pipe, looking at Neal through the smoke. Then he added: "You think you've got trouble. Well, I've got some, too. I can't do nothing but sit here and wait for them two buzzards to clean out their safe and run. Just knowing what they're gonna do ain't enough to arrest 'em for."

"Let's go get a drink," Neal said.

"I need one, all right," Rolfe said, "but I've got some advice to give you before I forget it. Stay out of trouble. You'll get yourself killed the way you're going. It's my guess Darley and Shelton will fly the coop before long. When they do, I'll need you. Nobody else I can count on."

Neal was silent until they went into O'Hara's bar. Bishop and Earl glanced at Neal, finished their drinks, and walked out.

Neal said: "I must smell pretty bad."

"I've got the same stink on me," Rolfe said. "Same with Doc.

He was telling me the other day that for the last three months he's had about half the calls he had a year ago. Anybody who can travel goes to Prineville." He motioned toward O'Hara. "Whiskey."

"The same," Neal said.

O'Hara waddled toward them, set a bottle and two glasses in front of them, then leaned forward, fat hands palm down on the bar. "You two and Doc Santee have bucked Darley from the first. Nobody can figure out why. It ain't as if they was taking water out of the river and maybe coming up short. Or spending money to build a reservoir. It's a sure fire proposition, with Darley giving us a chance to make a profit on our investment. All he's trying to do is to develop the community and give homes to a hundred families."

O'Hara straightened, wiped his hands on his apron, and pointed a finger at Neal. "You're the one that's stopping it. Darley was saying just this morning that they don't need more'n another ten thousand to start work. Your bank could loan that much without hurting nobody. I've tried to borrow a little. . . ."

"Sure, I know, O'Hara," Neal broke in. "I'm the dog in the manger."

For a time they glared at each other across the bar, Neal fighting an impulse to grab the saloon man by his fat neck and shake some sense into him. But he hadn't knocked any sense into Alec Tuttle. He wouldn't do any better with O'Hara.

"You're a hell of a lot worse'n a dog in a manger," O'Hara muttered, and, walking to the other end of the bar, began polishing glasses.

For a moment Neal stared at his drink. He wondered, as he had so many times, how much a man could take before he went crazy or killed somebody or ran away.

"I've known O'Hara for years," he said, "but he'd rather believe a crook who came here six months ago than me."

"You can savvy why they feel that way . . . O'Hara and Manion and all of 'em," Rolfe said. "They know the irrigation companies along the river have made money. Darley's promised 'em bigger profits with his deal because he's fixing to tap the lakes. Won't have the expense of building reservoirs. Just human nature to want something for nothing."

Neal nodded and took his drink. The sheriff's explanation didn't make it any easier. A solvent bank was as essential to the prosperity of a community as a fire department or a supply of drinking water. If he backed Darley and Shelton and the bank went broke, he'd be criticized more bitterly than he was now. On the other hand, if he made the loans that were being demanded, and then had to go to the law to collect what was owed, it would be worse.

Rolfe put his hand on Neal's shoulder. "I know how you feel, son. I've been in the same boat more'n once. So was your dad. You just can't please everybody. Take Sam, now. He was proud and pushy and bossy as hell, but he had some damned fine dreams. He used to say we'd have a town of fifteen thousand people here on the Deschutes, with a railroad coming up the river and sawmills slicing up the pines." He dropped his hand and turned to the bar again, adding: "You inherited them dreams along with the bank, boy. Don't lose 'em."

Neal threw a silver dollar on the bar. "My money good, O'Hara?"

"It's good," the saloon man said sullenly. "Any you let go of, I mean."

As Neal turned away, Rolfe said: "Hang and rattle. This'll break in a day or so. That's why you got that note, the way I figure."

Neal walked out. He wouldn't go back to the bank today. Henry Abel could handle anything that came up. He'd go home, saddle his horse, Redman, and take a ride to the Circle C. He had to get out of town, had to think, and somehow find a little peace of mind.

His fears and hatreds were all knotted up inside him so he couldn't even eat a meal without having it lie in his stomach like a rock. Maybe he ought to go to Doc Santee. No, it wouldn't do any good. What ailed him was too much for any pill-roller to cure, even a good one like Santee.

He walked with his head down, crossing the street and angling through the trees to the river. For a moment he paused, his gaze on the clear, swift moving stream. Maybe he ought to get Jane and Laurie out of town. If Joe Rolfe was right, it wouldn't be for more than a week at most. But then he'd have to tell Jane everything that had happened. And Laurie would be upset. No, it was better just to let it rock along.

He went on, leaving the river and walking rapidly along the dusty street to his house. He went in and closed the door softly, hoping that Jane and Laurie were gone, or that Laurie was at least asleep. He listened for a moment, hearing Jane's humming from the kitchen. Laurie must be out playing or taking a nap, or he'd hear her, for she was perpetually in motion when she was awake.

Crossing the parlor as quietly as he could, he climbed the stairs to his and Jane's bedroom, and, taking off his clothes that had been badly soiled, he put on another pair of pants and a flannel shirt, then buckled his gun belt around him, his bone-handled .44 in the holster.

He went into the bathroom, the only one in Cascade City. This was something else people talked about. They said he had plenty of money to spend on a zinc tub and a hot water tank, but, when it came to helping his neighbors out, he didn't have a nickel.

He stared at the mirror, thinking he had been lucky not to have his face cut up more than it was. He had bruises on his chin and under his left eye, but maybe Jane wouldn't notice.

The instant he stepped into the kitchen, Jane asked: "What are you doing home this time of day?" She looked at him and frowned. "Who'd you have a fight with?" Then she saw the gun on his hip, and cried out: "Neal, what are you doing with that six-shooter?"

She stood at the table, a paring knife in her hands. She had been peeling potatoes, but now she just stood looking at him, frightened and worried. He walked to her, thinking how much he loved her and how beautiful she was, even wearing an everyday house dress with a red-and-white checked apron, a dab of flour on one cheek.

He put his arms around her and kissed her. She dropped the paring knife and hugged him, returning his kiss with sweet, lingering warmth, telling him as she did every day when he came home that she loved him just as much as she had when they were married. Then she drew her head back, saying sternly: "Answer my questions, both of them."

"You're as pretty as a spotted heifer and I love you," he said, "and the world is full of trouble. We're going to let Henry Abel run the bank and we're moving back to the Circle C. Henry can decide who to make loans to and who not to."

He said it as if he were joking, but he was serious. The temptation had been a growing one for months. He was sure Jane would not object, but now, seeing how grave her face was, he wondered if he was wrong about her.

"I know the world is full of trouble," she said, "but I also know you never ran away from any of it. You're not going to now. I know you too well. You'll stay in that bank until your trouble with Darley and Shelton is settled. And you still haven't answered my questions."

"I had a ruckus with Darley." There was no reason to tell her about the note from Ed Shelly, he thought. "I'm going to take a

54

ride out to the ranch. Redman needs some exercise. So do I."

"But the gun. . . ."

"Just a precaution," he interrupted.

She sighed as if knowing he would not tell her more until he had to. But she wasn't ready to let him go. Her arms were still around him, her face close to his, and now he sensed that something was worrying her. She said—"Neal."—and stopped.

"I'll be back in time for supper," he said, "but, if you want to buy that new hat in Lizzie Arms's millinery shop, I guess our credit's good."

"Neal, stop it. I don't have to have a new hat every week like that Fay Darley." She bit her lower lip, then plunged on: "Neal, I can't help hearing gossip. About how folks feel because the bank isn't loaning money to invest with Darley. They hate you and they're saying terrible things. I'm afraid of what they'll do."

"I can take care of myself," he said, "but I'm worried about you and Laurie. You'd better be careful and keep a close watch on her." He kissed her and walked to the back door.

"Neal, you don't think they'd hurt Laurie because of this?"

He still didn't want to tell her about Ed Shelly's note, and he wasn't sure whether Joe Rolfe was right. The note could well have been a clumsy effort on Darley's and Shelton's part to make him so worried he'd stop fighting them, but there was a chance Ed Shelly was actually here, that he'd hired someone to slip that note into Neal's pocket.

Suddenly the terror of the nightmare was in him again, and he remembered how often he had dreamed that Ed Shelly was taking his revenge on Laurie or Jane. He said: "I don't know what they'll do. Just keep an eye on Laurie. Don't take any chances yourself, either."

He wheeled and left the house. He saddled his bay gelding and mounted, and, when he reached the edge of town, he put the horse into a run. But it didn't help. Nothing helped. He just couldn't shake the eight-year-old fear that Ed Shelly would somehow take a terrible revenge, a fear that now was brought into sharp focus because Ed Shelly was back. He must be. Now that he'd had time to think about it, Neal didn't believe that note was Ben Darley's trick.

CHAPTER SIX

A mile from town Neal noticed the remains of a campfire between the road and river. He dismounted and examined the ashes carefully, irritated and concerned. This was Circle C range, and both Neal and Curly Taylor, who was ramrodding the ranch now, discouraged saddle bums from camping here. This man was undoubtedly a saddle bum or he would have ridden on into town.

From the signs, Neal judged the fellow had been here two or three days. Neal walked back to his horse, wondering if there could be a connection between this man and the note from Ed Shelly. Or some connection with Darley and Shelton. Shrugging, he mounted and put his gelding up the slope east of the river, deciding he was jittery and imagining dangers that did not exist.

He took a switchback course to the top of the ridge, swinging back and forth between the barren outcroppings of lava. The horse's hoofs stirred the dust and pine cones and dry needles that had been here undisturbed for centuries. Once atop the ridge, he turned south, not stopping until he could look down upon the Circle C buildings.

Dismounting, he rolled and lighted a cigarette, hunkering down at the base of a pine. He often came here when the petty problems that stemmed from town living became so burdensome he could not stand it.

From this point Neal could see miles of the river, a band of silver shadowed by the pines that crowded both banks. On the other side were the snow-capped peaks of the Cascades, and to the east the pines gave way to junipers and sagebrush. Mountains, river, and high desert: these, to Neal Clark, were all a man needed to make his world complete.

Today the problems were far from petty, and Neal was unable to shake off the depressing feeling that trouble had only started for him. As he smoked, looking down at the Circle C, he thought how completely the stone ranch house symbolized his father. Huge and terribly permanent, it was the only kind of house Sam Clark would ever have thought of building.

Neal's father had lived in the big house very little, but apparently he had been happy for the short time he had been there, dreaming the big dreams Joe Rolfe had talked about in O'Hara's bar. Probably the thought never occurred to him that it was not the kind of house his son or his son's wife wanted.

At a time like this, in the silence broken only by the wind sounds as it rushed across the ridge, Neal could think of himself and his future, and Jane and Laurie, and of the many months Jane had lived in the stone house, forbidden to change anything, never allowed to feel it was really her home, and yet somehow managing to change it simply by being there. But if Sam Clark had felt the change, he certainly had never indicated it.

Now the old question that had plagued him long before his father died crowded back into Neal's mind. How far could a son go in letting his father dictate to him, either dead or alive? If Neal had had his choice, he'd have stayed right there on the Circle C, but, no, Sam Clark had decided Curly Taylor could run the outfit, and Neal and Jane must move to town.

Perhaps he had no reason to regret what he had done, for certainly Jane's life was easier in town than it had been on the ranch. But he didn't think that was important, for Jane was not a woman to choose an easy life. He knew that she would accept his choice without question. He had done pretty well with the bank, he thought, largely because Henry Abel had taught him what he had to know. The bank was in good shape, again largely because of Abel's conservative influence. Neal, according to Abel, was inclined to be soft.

This reminded Neal of what people thought about him. It was that, he knew, which had brought his feelings to a head and made him want to leave the bank. He took criticism far too hard, Abel told him. So had Joe Rolfe and Doc Santee.

But there was one vital point that never occurred to them. If Sam Clark were alive and running the bank, the men who hated Neal today would not have hated his father. Chances were the older Clark would have succeeded in chasing Darley and Shelton out of the country.

Neal could not fill Sam Clark's shoes. That was the rub. On the other hand, he didn't really want to. He had to be his own man. He had resisted his father on occasion and sometimes he had won his point, but he invariably had the feeling these were only temporary victories. In the long run, Sam Clark's will overpowered everything else. It was small comfort to realize he was not alone in this, that Joe Rolfe or Doc Santee or Henry Abel would have said the same thing.

Then, because his restlessness would not permit him to return to the confines of the town, he mounted and put Redman down the slope toward the ranch. He often felt this way, even before the Darley-Shelton business had come into sharp focus, and it convinced him that sooner or later he had to return to the ranch, that he could not and would not spend a lifetime in town. In that regard he had much of his father in him. Perhaps it was this very restlessness that had kept Sam Clark on the move and prevented him from being satisfied with anything he attained.

It was noon when he reached the ranch buildings, set in a clearing in the pines on the east side of the road. A log barn, outbuildings, innumerable corrals, all shadowed by the sprawling stone house that was now empty. Actually it was an ugly structure, for Sam Clark had built with an idea of permanence rather than beauty.

Neal put his horse into the corral and stood for a time, looking at the house. He remembered Jane saying that it sort of fitted the lava rock and the pines and the river across the road. If they returned, there were things she could do that would entirely change the appearance of the place. Curtains at the windows. Grass in front of the house. A few flowers that would grow in this climate. Lilacs, for instance, and some decorative trees such as weeping willows. It would be entirely different than when Sam Clark was alive.

Neal went into the cook shack and talked to the cook. Later, he had dinner with him and asked him to tell Curly Taylor about the saddle bum who had camped on the river above town. After that he went into the house. It was cold, for it had been shut up for weeks. Occasionally he brought Jane and Laurie out here for Sunday, but it had been quite a while since he had even done that.

For a time Neal stood in front of the fireplace that made up most of one wall. Pictures of his father and mother in gaudy, gilt frames hung above the mantel. His mother had been young and pretty. She'd died when he was small, and he could barely remember her. She'd had a hard life, he thought, and that may have been the reason she'd died when she had. Sam Clark had been a poor man then, and that, Neal knew, might have been the cause of his father's driving ambition and restlessness.

He glanced around the big room at the massive black leather couch and chair, the enormous oak table in the middle of the room, the walnut bookcase, the floor bare of rugs. If they did come back, he thought, Jane could furnish the room as she saw fit. Certainly everything that was here now would go.

He walked into the small room that had served as his father's office. Now it was Curly Taylor's. Neal smiled at the tally books, the box of .45 shells, and a bridle that lay on the spur-scarred desk. He glanced around at the saddle and guns and odds and ends of leather and the rest of the stuff Taylor had succeeded in gathering. The room was a boar's nest, totally different from the orderly office Sam Clark had kept, but now it seemed a friendly room. Neal was shocked by the implications of that thought and, swinging around, walked out of the room and the house.

He saddled his horse, but he didn't mount for a time. He stood beside his gelding, a hand on the horn, his eyes on the house. The restlessness had died in him. He was ready to go back to town, to face whatever must be faced. He couldn't run away from either the ranch or the bank, or the problems that faced him.

It wasn't important what his father would have done or how people would have responded to his father. It wasn't even important whether he filled his father's shoes; it was important that he fill his own. He had charted his course and he could not change, even if it meant danger to Jane or Laurie.

He mounted and rode away, relieved and still vaguely uneasy when his thoughts fastened again upon Ed Shelly and the note he'd found in his pocket. He was so lost in his thoughts that he did not see Fay Darley standing between the road and the river until she called: "Good afternoon, Mister Clark!"

He reined up, startled. She stood holding the reins of a livery-stable mare, smiling in the provocative way she had. She was wearing a black riding skirt and a leather jacket and a flat-topped Stetson that was tilted rakishly on one side of her head. She stood with her legs spread so that Neal could see her ankles, the skirt molded against her thighs, and again that titillating sense of excitement flooded him as it had every time he had seen her.

He touched his hat. "Good afternoon, Missus Darley."

He would have ridden on if she had not said: "Will you get down for a moment, Mister Clark? I realize this seems bold, and I suppose it is, but the truth is I've been waiting for you. I knew you had left town and that you'd come along the road sooner or later, so I waited."

She must have been waiting for a long time, he thought. Nothing but trouble could come from having anything to do with this woman, but he stepped down, rationalizing that any other man would have done the same.

"I'm glad you waited," he said. "I've got a question to ask you."

She looked at him warily, then said: "I'll be happy if the question is what I hope it is. A man is supposed to do the pursuing, but I learned long ago that there are times when a woman must let her heart speak or she will always regret it."

She was a beautiful and experienced woman, and he was both attracted and repelled by her. He didn't understand the latter unless he was afraid of her. He glanced at her, then looked down, scraping a toe through the dust of the road.

"You're wrong, ma'am," he said. "About the question."

"Am I?" she asked softly, paused, and then said: "Did you have trouble with Ben?" She dropped the reins and, walking to Neal, gently touched the bruise on the side of his face. "I warned you. He'd kill me if he knew I had spoken to you."

"I reckon he wouldn't go that far." He glanced at her and lowered his gaze again. "Anyhow, he got the worst of it."

"I'm glad," she said spitefully. "I hope you busted him good. He's bad. So's Shelton. I wish you'd leave for a while. They're arousing people against you. If you stay, they'll hang you."

So that was the game! He should have known. Darley had sent her out here to wait for him in the hopes he could be scared out of town, then they'd be free of the man who had partially blocked them. He met her gaze, thinking that now he knew her for exactly what she was.

"I'd say you were trying to get me out of town for some reason you haven't told me," he said.

"That's right. It's the reason your life is in danger and why you've got to leave tonight. A man named Stacey is coming in on the stage from Portland in the morning. That's why Ben has stayed here as long as he has. He believes he can persuade Stacey to invest ten thousand dollars in the project. He realizes he's gambling against time, but, with you out of town, he's convinced he's got a sure thing."

"It's safer to get me to leave town than to kill me," Neal said. "That it?"

"That's right," she said with honesty he didn't expect, "but what you don't know is that I'll be saving your life. I'm leaving Ben no matter what happens to you." She licked her lips with the tip of her tongue, her eyes not leaving his face, then she added: "A woman has to dream, Neal, or she'd go crazy. I've done my share of dreaming since I came to Cascade City. About you."

She stood with her hands at her sides, her breasts rising and falling with her breathing. The calm cloak of efficiency that she wore in Ben Darley's office was not on her now. To him she seemed a young, wistful girl, hoping for something from life that she did not actually believe she would ever have. That made him a fool for even thinking it, he told himself, for she was anything but young and wistful.

Then he remembered the note he had found in his pocket. It was the question he had meant to ask when he'd first dismounted, and had been sidetracked. Now he said roughly: "Maybe you'd like to tell me how that note got into my pocket this afternoon."

Wide-eyed, she asked: "What note?"

"From Ed Shelly. It said he hadn't forgotten what happened to his brother and father."

"Neal." She put her hands on his shoulders. "You don't think I had anything to do with putting it in your coat pocket? You . . . you can't."

"Who did?"

"I don't know," she said as if troubled by the question. "I didn't know there was a note, but Ben might have done it. Or Shelton. They know about your trouble with the Shelly gang. I heard them talking about trying to scare you out of town by using Ed Shelly's name, but I thought they gave up the idea." She shivered. "Neal, it might be true. Maybe someone around town really is Ed Shelly."

"Well, by God," a man said behind Neal. "If this ain't a purty sight. I thought you was a married man, Clark."

Neal whirled to face the man who had come up behind him. As he turned, Fay Darley cried—"Ruggles!"—as if the name were squeezed out of her. She ran to her mare and, mounting, rode toward town in a gallop.

Neal did not look at her, but stood staring at the stranger. He had never seen the man before. He was in his thirties, tall and very thin, with a sneering expression on his brown lips that told Neal how much filth there was in his mind.

"Your name Ruggles?" Neal asked.

"That's my handle." He walked toward Neal. "I've got a letter for you that a. . . ."

"You've been camping here?" Neal interrupted.

"Yeah."

"You're on Circle C range. Get to hell off of it. We don't allow saddle bums to hang around. Too many things can happen. A fire. Or you might get a notion to eat some Circle C beef." Neal motioned toward town. "There's a hotel. . . ."

"To hell with you and hotels," Ruggles said angrily. "You've got gall, telling me where I can camp and where I can't. But it's all right for you to meet Missus Darley out here in the brush. If I'd have waited, I'd have seen something purty damned. . . ."

Neal hit him, sending him spinning half around. Ruggles tried for his gun, but Neal let him have it again, a hard right to the side of his head that knocked him flat on his back. Neal bent over him and pulled his gun out of leather, then stepped back and shoved it under his waistband.

Ruggles lay on the ground, rubbing his face where Neal had hit him. He said: "I never forget a man who hits me. When I see you next time, I'll be heeled and don't you forget it." He pulled an envelope out of his pocket and held it out for Neal to take. "I'm broke, and a fellow in town hired me to give you this. I was gonna take it to your house, but I won't need to."

Neal took the letter and jammed it into his coat pocket. He said: "If you start any talk about me and Missus Darley, I'll kill you. Understand?"

"Yeah, I savvy," Ruggles said. "But you don't look like no hero to me. You got it turned around. Soon as I get me a gun, I'll start hunting you."

Neal mounted and rode toward town. He looked back once to see that Ruggles was on his feet, leaning against a pine tree. *Suppose the man did start some talk in town? What would he accomplish, and what would Mrs. Darley do? Maybe make the story bigger and worse,* Neal thought bitterly.

This probably was a put-up job from the first, with Ruggles working for Darley, and Mrs. Darley knowing he was here. It added up to more trouble, dirty trouble he didn't want to bring upon Jane. Now that it was too late, he wished he had gone on and not stopped to talk to Mrs. Darley.

Then another thought came to him, hitting him hard. *Could this Ruggles be Ed Shelly?*

CHAPTER SEVEN

Neal did not tear the envelope open until he was out of Ruggles's sight. He was not at all surprised when he read:

Yesterday has become today, Clark. You'll pay for the murder of my father and brother, and so will your wife and girl.

Ed Shelly

No, Neal wasn't surprised. It was making a pattern in his mind and he didn't like the looks of the pattern. Mrs. Darley begging him to leave town and giving him that hogwash about having done her share of dreaming about him since she'd been in Cascade City. She knew the stranger Ruggles by name. The hours she must have spent out there on the road south of town waiting for him to come home. Ruggles, too. Now he could spread a story about the respectable banker with a wife and child who had met Mrs. Darley out there along the river.

It was a pattern, all right, the dirty pattern set by men who didn't care how they pulled him down as long as they did it. Neal wasn't as concerned about this note as he had been earlier in the day when he received the first one. Ed Shelly was dead. He must be. Joe Rolfe had said so repeatedly and Neal had to believe it was true. Mrs. Darley had said that her husband and Shelton knew about his trouble with the Shelly gang and had thought about using Ed Shelly's name to scare him out of town.

That was the whole thing in a nutshell. Mrs. Darley had been honest with him to a point. She had mentioned a man named

66

Stacey who was coming to town and had $10,000 to invest. Any sane man coming to Cascade City under those conditions would first of all go to the local banker for an opinion, so Darley and Shelton would do everything they could to get him out of town before Stacey arrived. They weren't done, either, and they wouldn't be done until he was gone or they were in jail, or they were dead.

He rode back to town slowly, arriving at his barn at supper time. He pulled gear from Redman and watered and fed him, then, stepping into the runway, he was reminded of the gun under his waistband that he had taken from Ruggles. He didn't want Jane to see it, or to know about what had happened, so he took a look at it—a walnut-handled .45, a good gun with a fine balance that might indicate Ruggles was a professional gunslinger brought here to kill him.

In a sudden flurry of anger, he tossed the gun into the manger of a vacant stall and, walking behind Jane's mare, left the barn. He stopped, remembering that both Mrs. Darley and Ruggles had been waiting for him beside the road, so they had known he was out of town and would probably return on the road. That meant, then, that they'd had him under observation all day, and undoubtedly many days before this because they knew his habits. He rode to the Circle C often, invariably following the same route that he had today.

Suddenly he realized that it didn't make any difference whether it was actually Ed Shelly signing these notes or not. The last one made a threat against Jane and Laurie. Darley and Shelton could be just as dangerous and ruthless as Ed Shelly had ever been.

He stood motionlessly, breathing hard, and fought for composure. He didn't want to go into the house and let Jane see him as thoroughly unnerved as he was now. He felt a sharp pain in the left part of his chest. It had been there before, but it was worse now. Nervous tension, Doc Santee had called it.

"It's not your heart," Doc had said a little testily, "so quit worrying about it."

Well, he wasn't worried about his heart. He wasn't even worried about himself. Jane's and Laurie's safety was enough to worry anyone. He could not understand how two men could be evil enough to work through a woman and child to control another man's actions, but now he was convinced that was exactly what was happening.

It could be only a bluff. Possibly it would be enough if he left town only for one day, just long enough to let Darley and Shelton fleece the new victim who would be here in the morning, but he couldn't do it. He was Sam Clark's son, and for all of Sam Clark's ambition, he had been a man who put duty first, and he had taught Neal to do the same.

Neal waited until he had regained his composure. Sooner or later he would have to tell Jane what had happened and what he feared, but he would put it off as long as he could.

When he stepped into the kitchen, Jane was pouring gravy into a bowl. The room was filled with the tangy odor of supper. He took a long, sniffing breath of appreciation.

"That's enough to make a man's mouth water until he's likely to drown," he said.

Jane looked at him, a question in her eyes. She knew him well, sometimes sensing his moods and troubles before he said a word about them. Now she was wondering why he had stayed away so long, he thought, but she didn't ask him.

"Go upstairs and wash, dear," she said, smiling. "It'll just be a minute."

He walked through the dining room past the table with its white linen cloth and napkins, the lighted candles and the good silver and the Ironwood plates. She was putting on a show for him tonight, he thought, something she seldom did, but she sensed how deeply his worry had cut into him the last few days, and this was her effort to take his mind off his troubles.

He went on through the parlor and up the stairs to the bathroom where he washed. When he came back downstairs, Laurie had come in from the yard. She squealed—"Daddy!"— and ran to him. He picked her up and held her high while she kicked and kept on squealing: "Daddy, Daddy, you've been gone all day!"

He brought her to him and hugged her, and she kissed him and put her arms around his neck. Jane came in from the dining room and stood smiling at them. She said: "Supper's ready." He put Laurie down and she ran to her chair at the table. Neal swallowed, fighting the lump in his throat. Nothing could happen to them, he told himself. Nothing! He wouldn't let it.

Laurie chattered while they ate, with Jane nodding and answering her questions. Neal didn't say anything. He didn't feel like it. He only knew he could not go on this way, torn by these fears for Jane and Laurie, and all the other worries that had come to him through these last months. He had let it go too long. He'd see Darley after supper and get the truth out of him if he had to beat him to death. If Shelton interfered, he'd kill him.

After they finished eating, Laurie said in a commanding voice: "I want a story, Daddy."

"She's been playing outside all day," Jane said. "Why don't you put her to bed, Neal?"

He nodded, and rose.

"I want a ride," Laurie said in that same commanding tone. "Piggy-back."

Jane laughed. "You'd think she was the crown princess, the way she gives orders."

"What's a crown princess, Daddy?" Laurie demanded.

Neal looked down at her, fighting again for composure. He had always known how much he loved her, but now it was hammered home to him with terrible, devastating force. She was a strange child in many ways—delicate features, small for her age, and very shy with strangers—but she was strong and healthy and got along unusually well with the other children in the neighborhood. She was curious about everything; her question about a crown princess was typical of her.

"Well," Neal said, "I guess a crown princess is a princess with a crown on her head."

Laurie considered the answer for a moment, then she said: "I'd like to see one, a big crown with lots of diamonds."

Jane laughed. "So would I, honey. Run along, both of you."

Neal gave her a piggy-back ride to her bedroom, undressed her, and put her to bed, then he sat down on the side of the bed and told her the story of Cinderella, which was her favorite. Then he tucked the covers around her shoulders, kissed her good night, and blew out the lamp.

"Go to sleep now," he said.

She yawned. "I will, Daddy."

He walked to the door; the lamp in the hall shone into the room. He stood there a moment, looking back at her. She yawned again. She said: "Good night, Daddy." He said—"Good night, Princess."—and closed the door.

He had reached the parlor when he heard the doorbell. He hesitated, then he heard Jane coming from the kitchen.

"I'll get it!" he called, and hurried across the room and into the hall. Then he paused again, uneasiness making a prickle along his spine. It could be Ruggles. Maybe the man had got a gun from Darley or Shelton.

Neal drew his pistol, hoping that it was Ruggles and he could get it over with. Holding the gun in his right hand, Neal flung the front door open. No one was in sight. Then he saw the

envelope on the threshold. Stooping, he picked it up, not doubt-
ing at all what he would find.

He stepped inside, closed the door, and slipped his gun back
into leather. He tore open the end of the envelope, took out the
sheet of paper, and, unfolding it, held it up to the bracket lamp
on the wall. The note was printed with a dull pencil the same as
the others.

*After waiting eight years, Clark, I won't forget you. I'll make
you suffer like you made me suffer. I'm going to get Laurie.*

Ed Shelly

He crushed the envelope and note into a wad and shoved it
into his pocket. He leaned against the wall, his eyes closed.
Three times within a matter of hours. He had been so sure this
was Darley's and Shelton's way of getting him out of town.
Now he wasn't certain. A terrifying thought crept into his mind
again.

Suppose this crazy man Ruggles was really Ed Shelly who
had come back for revenge? Instead of Darley hiring Ruggles,
maybe Ruggles had hired Mrs. Darley or Shelton or someone
else to drop the first note into his pocket. If he followed this
line of reasoning, he could reach only one conclusion. These
notes had nothing to do with Darley and Shelton's irrigation
scheme and their plan to trim Stacey when he reached town
tomorrow.

He had to find out, some way. He didn't know who to fight
until he did. It was the uncertainty more than anything else that
was bothering him. But how was he going to find out? He
thought of Jane and Laurie again. Fear took possession of him,
in his belly, in the crawling tingle that worked down his spine,
in a desperate rump-tingling feeling he had never experienced
before.

The doorbell rang again, giving him a start and setting his

heart to pounding again. He yanked his gun from the holster and jerked the door open, fully expecting to see Ruggles. Or Darley or Shelton. He was frantic enough to expect anything, but it was Henry Abel standing there, looking more tired and worried than Neal had ever seen him.

"Come in, Henry." Neal holstered his gun. "Come on in. Jane's probably got some coffee left from supper."

"I'd like to, Neal, but I can't," Abel said. "I haven't been home yet, and Lena will raise hell. What was the gun for?"

"I'm just jumpy, I guess. You can come in for a minute."

"I'd like to, but I can't," Abel said. "I stopped at O'Hara's for a drink and kind of ran into something. A lot of men were there. Quinn, Olly Earl, Jud Manion, Tuttle. All that bunch. They pushed me around a little, trying to make me promise I'd talk to you about changing the bank's policy."

Neal stepped outside and put a hand on Abel's shoulder. He was not a strong man physically and Neal had never thought of him as being a brave one, but he suddenly realized that no one could judge courage in anyone else.

"What did you tell them, Henry?"

Abel grimaced. "Nothing. How could I? I don't own the bank. I don't determine its policies."

Neat dropped his hand. He could have expected this. What Abel said was true, but what he hadn't said was that his judgment went a long way with Neal. If he had not been so convinced right along that the wise thing was for the bank to refuse all loans at this time, Neal might not have been as firm in his policy as he had been.

"That what you came to tell me?" Neal asked.

"No," Abel said. "I'm scared. You see, they're doing some talking about you. You don't realize how they hate you. They blame everything on you because Darley says he needs just a little more money to start work. It's the same old talk with just

72

one difference. Now they're threatening to lynch you. They mean it, Neal. They're just crazy enough to mean it."

"With me out of the way, you'd be running the bank," Neal said. "They figure they can manage you. That it?"

Abel's face turned red. "I guess a man who's as scared of his wife as I am hasn't much right to claim he'll stand on his convictions, but I will." He shrugged. "Hell, Neal, that's not the point. You've got me, the sheriff, and Doc Santee on your side. That's all. You know how a mob starts. Some drinking and some talk, and then it's out of hand. What are you going to do?"

"Nothing right now," Neal said, feeling a great flood of relief. "To tell you the truth, Henry, I hope they come after me. I need to fight somebody . . . somebody I can get my teeth into, not somebody that's like a handful of fog."

Abel looked at him and shook his head. "You're crazy, Neal. Clear, clean crazy." He whirled and disappeared into the darkness.

Neal stepped into the house and shut the door. Abel was right. His talk had been crazy. The situation couldn't be changed by fighting his neighbors. He returned to the parlor, wondering if there was anything to this lynch talk. He was afraid there was.

CHAPTER EIGHT

Neal pulled the couch closer to the fireplace and sat down, his long legs stretched out toward the fire. He heard Jane putting things away in the kitchen, and then her steps as she crossed the dining room and came into the parlor.

"Neal," she said, "I want to know what you're keeping from me."

He looked up and tried to smile, but it wouldn't quite come off. "Nothing," he said. "I mean, nothing you don't already know."

She knelt beside him and put her head against his leg. "Who was at the door? I heard it ring twice."

"Henry," he said. "I'd been gone most of the day and there were some things he had to know about."

She was silent for a time. He didn't want to tell her anything else, not until he had to, anyway. This was something he had to fight out himself, or with Joe Rolfe's and Doc Santee's help. Not Jane's. His job was to protect her. There was nothing she could do but have faith in him and love him, but he didn't say that, for sweet words came hard for him.

"What about the second time," she said. "You might just as well tell me. I'm going to keep after you till you do."

"Henry was the second time."

"The first time, then?"

"Some prank, I guess. Nobody was there when I opened the door."

She looked up at him, her jaw set stubbornly. "Neal, we've got to talk. You don't make it easy. You've got a little of the flint that was in your dad, enough to make you pretty hard-headed sometimes."

He was irritated by that, but he was too tired to argue. He said: "I didn't get a chance to pick my father."

"Of course not. I'm just trying to say that you always keep me in one part of your heart, the nice, easy part. You let me share your triumphs and jokes and the good things that happen to you, but I never get a chance to share your troubles. I want to, Neal. This way you make me feel like I'm only half a wife to you."

He stared at her, hurt by what she'd said and wanting to strike back. He had enough trouble now without her adding to it by having her tell him he made her feel like half a wife. Then he saw the tenderness that was so plain to read in her face and the resentment left him.

"I don't mean to," he said, "but it's my job to take care of you."

She got up and, sitting down beside him, took one of his hands. "And it's my job to take care of you, too, as much as I can. Now you've got to tell me what happened today that's worrying you."

He hesitated, still not wanting to tell her and yet finding some justice in what she said. Maybe he did make her feel like half a wife, maybe there was more of Sam Clark in him than he realized. There had been times when he had felt like half a son, times when his father hadn't taken him into his confidence and he'd resented it just as Jane was resenting it now. Besides, and this was what decided him, he had to tell Jane about the notes so she would be careful with Laurie.

So he told her, beginning with Jud Manion's visit, told her everything except how he felt when he saw Fay Darley in the

75

company office, and again on the road beside the river, and the real reason for Henry Abel's visit.

"Well, it looks to me like Joe could do something," Jane said when he finished. "They must have a criminal record."

"They probably have," he agreed, "but chances are they've changed their names."

She was silent for a moment, her leg pressed against his, her hand squeezing his. He had never been a sentimental man, not in the way Jane would have liked for him to be. That again was proof there was a great deal of Sam Clark in him.

He could never remember his father showing any overt sign of affection for him. Right now was the time for sentiment, the time to tell her how much he loved her. There were a lot of things he should tell her, but he didn't say any of them.

"I guess the part I don't understand is why men like Jud don't trust your judgment," she said. "They would have believed your father."

"That's what hurts," he said. "I'm young, and haven't been proved, I suppose. Darley's smart in putting it on a community basis. He's promised that the men who bought stock will have a chance to work in the ditch, so they'll have money to spend in O'Hara's bar and Quinn's store. The company will buy horses from the livery stable and equipment from Olly Earl. I can't say anything except that I'm saving them money when I won't make the loans they want. Darley twists that around by making it look as if I'm sore because I can't hog the profit."

"Neal, don't worry about those notes," she said. "They're probably just bluff, but I'll stay in the house tomorrow and keep Laurie in, just in case."

"My Thirty-Eight is in the bureau," Neal said. "Better keep it handy tomorrow."

She nodded agreement and, putting a hand under his chin, tipped his head back and kissed him, her lips hungry for his and holding them for a long moment. Then she rose. "I'm going to bed. Are you going to sit up?"

He nodded. "Don't stay awake for me. I couldn't go to sleep now if I went to bed."

"You're tired, Neal." She hesitated, then murmured: "Good night, darling."

"Good night," he said. He watched until she was halfway up the stairs, then he called: "Jane!"

She stopped and looked back over her shoulder. "What is it, Neal?"

"I was just thinking," he said. "I may go out and take a walk. I feel like a clock that's been wound too tight. I'll lock both doors, but maybe you'd better put that Thirty-Eight under your pillow."

"All right, Neal," she said, and went on up to their room.

He heard the bedroom door close, then the silence was tight and oppressive. He smoked one cigarette after another, impatience goading him, but he couldn't think of anything to do. He felt like a duck sitting on a lake, his enemies in position to shoot at him, but he wasn't in position to shoot back because he didn't know who to shoot at.

He thought of the lynch talk Henry Abel had brought to him, and suddenly a crazy fury took hold of him. He'd call every one of those money-hungry bastards into the bank tomorrow and loan them all they wanted. Let them give their money to a couple of thieving con men, and, when the time came, he'd close them out to the last man. By God, there had to be an end to what you did for other people, trying to save them from themselves.

The fury lasted only for a moment. He thought again of his father as he had so many times these last days as the pressure had mounted. Tough, domineering, hard-headed, Sam Clark was a strange mixture, but he'd had some good traits. If he were alive today, he would have said the same thing to Jud Manion that Neal had. No matter how much he would have been threatened or hated, or how much a man like Ed Shelly, appearing from an eight-year-old yesterday, worried him, Sam Clark would have stuck to his guns.

Some of the flint that had been in his father had come down to him, Jane had said. *Not all of it,* Neal thought, *but enough.* That thought closed the door to any easy avenue of escape. He'd see it through; the bank would hold to the policy that he and Henry Abel had decided upon.

The clock on the mantel struck midnight. Neal rose and threw more wood on the fire. He had a strange feeling of detachment about all of this, as if he were a sponge that had been completely saturated and could hold no more.

Then, because he had to do something, he decided to get Joe Rolfe out of bed and talk to him. The old sheriff was pretty cantankerous at times and he wouldn't like it, but Neal had to talk to someone and the only choice he had was between Rolfe and Doc Santee. He didn't want to bother Doc, who often had too little chance to sleep at best.

He locked the kitchen door, thinking that he and Jane would not attempt to control Laurie's life as his had been controlled. Laurie! If anything did happen to her. . . . He went upstairs, driven by a compulsion he could not control.

Jane had left a lamp burning in the bracket on the hall wall. Laurie's door was ajar. Gently he pushed it open and stepped into the room. There was no possible way for anyone to get into her room except by coming up the stairs and along the hall just as he had done. No one had gone past him. He had been in the parlor from the time Laurie had gone to bed, or in the hall, or back in the kitchen.

She was all right. She had to be. Nothing could have happened to her. But he could not see her in the thin light that fell through the door from the hall. Suddenly panicky, he ran across the room to the bed, the horrible fear that she was gone taking breath out of his lungs as sharply as if he'd been hit in the stomach.

He stopped at the side of her bed, breathing hard. She lay next to the wall on the far edge, almost hidden under the covers. For a time he stood motionlessly, shocked by what this moment of crazy panic had shown him.

He could barely make out her face and blonde hair against the pillow in the near darkness. Needing reassurance, he struck a match and leaned over her bed. She was all right, her small face sweetened by a half smile. Jane often said that Laurie talked to the angels when she was asleep. Shaking the match out, Neal told himself that she was not only talking to them; she was one of them.

No one else was as important to him as Laurie. Not even Jane. Certainly not his own life. He had known that all the time, but it took this moment of terror to make him fully realize it. He crumpled the charred remainder of the match between thumb and forefinger, fighting an impulse to reach down and take her into his arms.

If he woke her, she would sense the fear that was in him, and he would only alarm her, doing no good at all. Jane had done a fine job with Laurie, particularly in regard to fear. The child never fussed about going to bed or being left in the dark. Whatever happened, Laurie must not know about this threat against her.

He should go, he knew. Still, he lingered beside the bed, thinking how much Jane wanted other children, but, after Laurie's birth, Doc Santee had said the chances were slim that she would ever have another. For that reason Laurie meant more to both of them than she would under other circumstances. This was the most important thing in life, he thought, having a part of you perpetuated, gaining in that way the immortality that childless people could not have.

Reluctantly he turned and left the room, leaving her door open so Jane could hear her if she cried out. He felt a weakness in himself he had never felt before, a weakness that stemmed from the fact his most important possession was at stake, but the threat came from an enemy that was unknown except by these mysterious notes, an unknown that was vague and shapeless and terrifying.

He crossed the parlor to the hall, feeling a greater need than ever to see Joe Rolfe. The sheriff had an ageless quality, a capacity for giving confidence to those around him. Right now that was what Neal needed.

He put on his hat and sheepskin and went outside, leaving the hall lamp lighted. The thought occurred to him that for a moment he would be silhouetted against the light and he would make a perfect target. Still, the possibility of danger seemed remote until he heard the shot and saw the flash of flame from the far corner of the yard, the bullet slapping into the wall just above his head.

CHAPTER NINE

Neal dived headlong across the porch and stumbled and fell into the yard as another shot slammed out from that far corner, this one missing by a good five feet. He yanked his gun from holster and fired three times and rolled to a new position. He had nothing to shoot at except the spot where the ambusher had stood. The fellow wouldn't remain there, of course. A moment later he heard retreating footsteps as the man ran up the street.

For a time Neal did not move, aware there might be other men waiting. He heard someone inside the house, then Jane's voice: "Neal! You all right, Neal?"

"I'm all right. Blow out the hall lamp."

The hall went black, and Neal rose and slipped the gun into leather. No one else in the block had been aroused by the shooting. At least he saw no indication of it. Gunfire was not an uncommon thing this time of night, for O'Hara's bar stayed open until midnight or later, and cowboys often expressed themselves by emptying their guns as they rode out of town.

Neal went back to the house and closed the door. The lamp in the parlor was still lighted. He saw Jane standing in the hall, wearing nothing but her nightgown; the .38 he had left on the bureau in their bedroom was in her hand. Laurie was crying.

Neal said: "Tell her it was just some crazy cowboys riding home."

Jane nodded and ran up the stairs. A minute or two later Jane

81

returned. "She's all right. She said she wished those cowboys would go home." Jane tried to smile, but she couldn't control her lips and they began to tremble.

Neal went to her and put his arms around her. "It's all right. I just got a scare. That's all. Funny thing. Just as I went outside, I thought it would be a good time for someone to take a pot shot at me, and then it happened."

Jane had buried her face against his chest. "Do you suppose it was that man, Ruggles, you had trouble with today?"

"Could have been. Or it might have been Darley or Shelton." Neal started to say Jud Manion or Tuttle or some of the townsmen, but didn't. It would only alarm her more if she knew how they felt, that lynch talk had been going around. Besides, they weren't the kind to bushwhack a man, so he said: "You go on back to bed. That fellow's gone for good."

Jane drew back, a muscle in her cheek twitching with the regularity of a pulse beat. She whispered: "I'm scared, Neal."

"I've got to see Joe," Neal said. "You'll be all right. Keep the doors locked. I'll lock the front one when I leave. Blow out the lamp in the parlor. I don't want any light showing when I go out this time."

He waited with his hand on the knob of the front door until the hall was dark, his hand on the butt of his gun. He had told Jane the bushwhacker wouldn't be back, but he wasn't as sure as he'd sounded. The man who had shot at him might have returned, or there might be another one waiting.

He eased outside, shut the door, and locked it. Then he stood motionlessly for several minutes, listening for sounds that were not natural for this late hour, eyes probing the night for any hint of movement. There was none, just the darkness relieved slightly by the star shine. He couldn't stay here all night, he thought, and left the porch. Walking fast, he went down the path to the street and turned toward the east corner of the block. From there he started climbing the hill to Joe Rolfe's house.

The sheriff lived alone on the crest above the river. This part of the town had never been planned. The houses were scattered haphazardly among the pines and lava outcroppings, and the street, following the lines of least resistance, twisted and squirmed to avoid those same trees and upthrusts of lava.

All of the houses in this part of town were dark, there were no street lamps, and more than once Neal came close to bumping into a clothesline or stumbling over a ledge of lava. He walked more cautiously, taking a good ten minutes to reach Rolfe's house. It seemed to him, with his sense of time completely distorted, that another ten minutes passed before his pounding brought Rolfe's sleepy yell: "I'm a-coming! Leave the damned door on its hinges, will you?"

A moment later Rolfe opened the door, a lamp in one hand. He was bare-footed, his pants hastily pulled over his drawers, and held up by one suspender, the other dangling below his waist. He squinted at Neal, hair disheveled, his mind not entirely freed of the cobwebs of sleep.

"Hell, I might've knowed it'd be you," he grumbled. "If there's another man in the county who can get into trouble up to his neck like you, I don't know who it is. Come on in."

As Neal stepped through the door, Rolfe said: "Trouble is you woke me out of the best dream I've had in twenty year. Purty girls swarming all over the place, and me reaching for 'em and never quite getting hold of one of 'em." Suddenly he sensed from the grim expression on Neal's face that something serious had happened. "Let's have it, son. Getting so I rattle on like a buggy that ain't been greased since Noah set the ark down on Mount Ararat."

"Somebody took a couple of shots at me when I left the house a while ago," Neal said.

"The hell." Rolfe sat down and stared at Neal. "I didn't think it would go that far. I sure didn't."

"That's not even a beginning." Neal handed him the note Ruggles had given him, told him what had happened, then gave him the last note that had been shoved under the door. Rolfe read it, shook his head as if he didn't believe it, and began to curse.

"What kind of a damn' fool proposition is this?" Rolfe shouted. "No sane man would lay a hand on a child. . . ." He stopped and gestured as if to thrust those words into oblivion. "I know what you're fixing to say. We ain't dealing with a sane man, and, by God, I think you're right."

"That makes it worse," Neal said. "I'm beginning to think Ed Shelly isn't dead like you've been claiming."

Rolfe pulled at his mustache thoughtfully, then he asked: "How old a man was this Ruggles?"

"Thirty-five maybe."

"If Ed Shelly was alive, he'd be just about your age. Not more'n twenty-seven at the most. Shelton and Darley are both older'n that. Besides, Ed was small. You'll remember you thought he was a half-grown kid. Well, he was about nineteen, and a boy ain't gonna grow much after he's that old. Darley and Shelton are too tall, and you claim this Ruggles gent is likewise tall."

Neal nodded. "A regular splinter."

"There you are. It ain't none of them three, and the chances of another stranger hanging around and nobody seeing him is mighty slim."

"You heard of Ruggles?"

"Yep. I seen him in O'Hara's bar. Reckon it was him, the way you describe him, but I didn't know he was camped on your range. I figured he was just a drifter riding through."

"What are you going to do?"

"Do! Maybe you can tell me." Rolfe looked at the note that threatened Laurie. "Your girl's safe enough tonight, I reckon. Jane's got a gun?" Neal nodded, and Rolfe went on: "It'll be different tomorrow when she's out playing. If this bastard that calls himself Ed Shelly is half-cracked, there's no way to tell what he'll do."

"Darley wants me out of town on account of the man they've got coming in on the stage from Portland," Neal said. "I've got my doubts that anybody's half-cracked. I think it's all hooked together. They're smart, Joe, sneaky smart."

"Could be the shooting was done to scare you," Rolfe said. "A real good shot . . . and I figure Shelton is . . . could lay that first bullet in close, aiming to miss. He was just waiting for you, chances are, knowing that, when you got the last note, you'd come after me sooner or later."

"Ruggles," Neal said thoughtfully, the name jogging his memory. "You know, Missus Darley knew him. What does that prove?"

"Nothing that I know of," Rolfe said blankly. "What are you getting at?"

"That there's some kind of a tie-up between him and Darley and Shelton. Of course we know that, but suppose we can prove it? Prove that one of them hired Ruggles to get that note to me?"

"Sure, it'd look bad," Rolfe conceded, "but I don't know how we can prove anything of the sort."

"Maybe Ruggles came to town after dark," Neal said, "and told Shelton what had happened. He might be bunking with Shelton tonight. He wouldn't go to Darley because Darley and his wife are at Tucker's boarding house, but Shelton sleeps alone in their office."

"You're just grabbing at a handful of straws," Rolfe said, "but I wouldn't mind putting the screws on that bastard. We've been too easy on him and Darley both. Let's go wake him up and listen to him squirm. Wait'll I get my shirt and boots on."

CHAPTER TEN

Neal walked beside Joe Rolfe down the twisting street toward the business block, the pines giant spears pointing at the dark sky, the lava rock low mounds among the earthbound shadows. They moved cautiously, but still stumbled over the lava outcroppings that edged sharply into the street. They would have fallen if they had not been walking slowly.

"Should have fetched a lantern," Rolfe muttered, when they reached Main Street. "I damn' near break my neck every time I come down that street after dark."

Neal said nothing. He had thought about a lantern, but decided against suggesting they bring one. On a night as dark as this a moving lantern would be as noticeable as a bright star in a black sky. Neal had a hunch Shelton expected him to do the very thing he was doing. If Shelton was watching from a window, a lantern would warn him, perhaps show him there were two instead of one.

Now, in the ebb-tide hours of early morning, no light showed along Main Street, not even in O'Hara's bar or the hotel lobby. Neal had the weird impression the town was deserted. It seemed to him that the sharp sound of boot heels on the boards of the walk echoed and reëchoed, the staccato beat inordinately slow to die in the otherwise silent night.

When they reached the foot of the stairs that led to the Darley and Shelton office over the Mercantile, Neal said: "Let me do the talking, Joe."

"Why?" Rolfe demanded.

"If he hears my voice and thinks I'm alone," Neal answered, "he'll tip his hand, but he'll play it close to his chest if he knows you're here."

Rolfe considered this for a moment, then he said: "All right, Neal, we'll play it your way."

Neal climbed the stairs, making no effort to be silent. Rolfe followed two steps behind him. Neal wondered if Shelton was asleep. Or was he sitting up expecting this visit? And did Darley know about the notes, or was it just Shelton's idea? Or was it either one of them? A lot of questions and no answers, but maybe they'd have some soon.

Standing beside the door, he pounded on it. One short moment of silence, then gunfire broke out from inside the company office, bullets slicing through the door and slapping into the wall across the hall. No warning, no demand for the visitor to identify himself. Nothing but the sudden burst of gunfire.

If Neal had been standing directly in front of the door, he'd have been hit. He drew his gun and fired, checking himself after the third shot as he realized he wasn't accomplishing anything. Shelton would not be foolish enough to remain in an exposed position on the other side of the door.

Then, after the last echo of the shots had faded, Neal was aware that Rolfe was not standing on the stairs behind him. He backed up, calling: "Joe?"

"Here," Rolfe said. "I got tagged."

The sheriff was halfway down the stairs when Neal reached him. Neal asked: "Where'd you get it?"

"In the arm. Just took off a hunk of hide."

"We'll get Doc up."

"No such thing. . . ."

"Come on, come on," Neal said impatiently.

He was thoroughly angry, now that he'd had time to think

about it. Not a word had been spoken. Whoever was in the of-fice—and it must be Shelton—had cut loose the instant he'd heard Neal's knock.

By the time Neal and Rolfe reached the street, lights had bloomed in the hotel lobby, Doc Santee's office, and O'Hara's bar. Before they reached the doctor's office, doors were flung open and men ran into the street, some in their underclothes, others hastily pulling on their pants, fingers fumbling with but-tons.

Someone yelled: "What happened?"

And another man: "Who got shot?"

The last was O'Hara's voice. Neal called: "Shelton tried to shoot me and the sheriff!" They were in front of Santee's office then. The doctor stood in the doorway, his bulky body almost filling it, with the lamp behind him throwing a long shadow across the boardwalk. Neal said: "Joe's hit, Doc."

"Fetch him in," Santee said, and swung around, content to ask questions later.

But the others had to know. O'Hara crowded into the office, Harvey Quinn shoving him forward. Olly Earl was a step behind them.

O'Hara asked: "What happened, Clark?"

Santee had taken Rolfe into his back room. Neal did not fol-low, but stood looking at the men who formed a solid wedge in the doorway. Others had joined them. Six altogether. Now seven. No, eight as the Sorrenson kid who worked nights in the livery stable appeared in the rear.

Neal saw no trace of friendliness in their faces, only hostility. That was exactly what he expected. He remembered what Dar-ley had said that afternoon: *People don't like you. Before this is over, they'll hang you.* It would take very little, he thought, to turn these eight men into a lynch mob. Henry Abel had been right.

"Damn it, you gonna answer me or not?" O'Hara shouted. "I asked you what happened."

"I went to the Darley and Shelton office with Joe Rolfe," Neal said. "We wanted to ask Shelton some questions, so I knocked on the door. Whoever was inside didn't say a word. Just started shooting. Must have been Shelton. Joe got nicked."

Still they stood there, staring at him truculently as if not believing he was telling it straight.

Finally Quinn asked: "Why would he do that?"

"Ask him."

"We will," O'Hara said, and, wheeling, motioned the others out of the doorway.

They were gone, O'Hara leading, the sound of their passage reminding Neal of the sullen departure of a storm. He stood in the doorway watching them, thinking how quickly the town had come to life. Only a few minutes before he'd had the impression it was deserted. Now it seethed with the strongest of human emotions: fear and greed and hate, violent emotions that could easily lead to death.

These men might be back with a rope for him. Was that what Shelton and Darley wanted? There was no way to know. How could you fathom a human mind that was as near the animal level as Shelton's? Or Darley's? Or both?

Turning, he walked across Santee's outer office to the back room, a little sick with fear. He would have no hesitation whatever if he had to shoot and kill Darley or Shelton. But he could not kill O'Hara or Olly Earl or the Sorrenson kid. Still, he would not be dragged out into the street with a rope on his neck.

Santee was putting a bandage on Rolfe's arm. He glanced up when Neal came in. He was a big, bald man with huge hands that were miraculously nimble for their size, and, like most doctors who served a vast area with a thin population, he was always tired and sleepy, for he spent more hours in the saddle than he did in bed.

"Joe'll have a sore arm for a while," Santee said. "He's staying here for the night. I'll give him something to make him sleep."

"The hell you will," Rolfe said angrily. "I'm going up there and drag Shelton out by his ear."

"You'll have a riot on your hands, if you do," Neal said. "The bunch that was here went to see him. You know what he'll tell them."

"No, I don't. Nothing he can say. Hell, he started throwing lead before. . . ."

"You'll wait till morning. They'll be cooled off by then." Santee picked up a bottle from a shelf, poured a drink, and handed it to Rolfe. "I'll tell you what he'll say if you don't know. He didn't hear your voice before you knocked on the door. That right, Joe?"

"Yeah, but. . . ."

"That's it in a nutshell. Shelton will claim he fired because he didn't know who was in the hall, but he had to protect the company money that was in the safe. He figured nobody would be pounding on the door this time of night unless it was a hold-up."

"That's the size of it," Neal said. "Doc, did Joe tell you about this Ruggles gent? And the notes I've been getting?"

"He told me," Santee said, "and I don't have any idea what it means, either, if that's what you want to know. But it doesn't seem reasonable for a man like Ruggles to be hanging around for the fun of it. And I don't think the notes are just a bluff."

"I'm scared," Neal said. "I'm so damned scared I don't know up from down. If Laurie's really in danger. . . ."

"Go home, Neal." Santee laid a hand on his shoulder. "Stay with Laurie. Keep her in the house."

"All right." Neal started to turn, then stopped. "Doc, would anybody but a crazy man think of using a child to get revenge?"

"You're thinking Ed Shelly is really around here?"

"It's possible."

"I don't think so," Santee said thoughtfully. "I'm convinced that Darley and Shelton will play every dirty, stinking trick they can to get you out of the country."

"But we don't know how far they'll go," Neal said, "so my question hasn't been answered. Would anyone but a crazy man hurt a child? It doesn't make any difference whether he's getting revenge or filling his pockets. A sane man just wouldn't use a child."

Santee reached for his pipe and filled it, scowling as he tamped the tobacco into the bowl. "Neal, I'm a doctor. I'm good at jobs like this." He nodded at Rolfe. "Or helping babies into the world." He tapped his forehead. "When it comes to saying whether a man is sane or crazy, well, I just don't know. All I know is that there's times when a crazy man acts sane, and vice versa."

"But if a man lives with his hate long enough. . . ."

"He can go crazy," Santee interrupted. "I'll agree to that, but our trouble is we're shooting in the dark. We don't know our man. If he is crazy, then Laurie's really in danger. All you can do is be damned sure she's never left alone."

"If you leave the house in the morning," Rolfe said, "be sure Jane keeps Laurie inside."

"She will," Neal said, and, turning, trudged wearily out of the office and along the boardwalk toward his home.

Neal walked through the pines, thinking that imaginary trouble can become real trouble within a matter of seconds. For eight years he had been plagued by his fear of Ed Shelly, his certainty the man would someday return. If he had not stepped into the street that day and shot Buck and Luke Shelly. . . .

But it was foolish to think about the might-have-beens. Not knowing even now whether Laurie and Jane were in real trouble or not, the only thing he could do was to take every precaution that was possible.

When he reached his house, he crossed the yard rapidly, his hand on gun butt, realizing that if Ruggles was the one who had shot at him before, the man might have returned. He unlocked the front door, opened it, and slipped inside. He closed and locked it, relieved. He leaned against the wall, breathing hard, and asking himself if he was being jumpy over nothing. He was a little ashamed, then thought he shouldn't be. The notes he'd received might be only bluffs, but the bullets that had been fired at him tonight were real indeed.

He lighted the lamp on the table in the parlor and went upstairs. He waited a moment outside his bedroom door, listening to Jane's even breathing, then went on to Laurie's room. The bracket lamp in the hall was lighted. He glanced in, saw that she was all right, and went back downstairs.

Drawing a chair in front of the fireplace, he threw on more wood, and then sat down to wait, his gun across his lap.

CHAPTER ELEVEN

Jane slept later than usual this morning. Ordinarily Neal got up half an hour before she did. It was his habit to build the fire, set the coffee pot on the front of the stove, then go to the woodshed and split the day's supply of wood. Jane would remain in bed, torn between the knowledge that she should get up and start breakfast, and the desire to linger in the comfortable warmth of the bed, enjoying a luxury she had never been able to afford when she and Neal had lived on the Circle C.

This morning she woke suddenly, the sharp April sunlight falling across her face from the east window. She had not slept well during the night, waking often and reaching to the other side of the bed to see if Neal was there. But he hadn't come. He wasn't there now, and suddenly she was afraid. Something must have happened to him or he would have come to bed hours ago.

The fear passed. If Neal had been hurt, she would have heard. Joe Rolfe or Doc Santee would have come to the house before this. Besides, she had faith in Neal's ability to handle any situation. He had always seemed indestructible to her. He still did, even though she realized he was more worried than he had ever been before in his life. He wasn't worried about himself, she knew. Being shot at last night had not bothered him as much as the warning notes that threatened her and Laurie.

Her thoughts went back to the early years of their marriage when Neal's father dominated everything they did. Sam Clark was the only man she had ever hated and she had been relieved when he died. Neal must have felt the same way, and instantly she knew she was wrong. In spite of all the things that were wrong with Sam Clark, Neal had never hated him.

She thought how helpless she had been on the ranch, just living and working and never having the slightest opportunity to do what she wanted to with the house. She had been tested as few wives were ever tested. Even moving to town had not been a free choice on Neal's part.

She got up and dressed, thinking that this trouble would be settled soon, today or maybe tomorrow. One good thing would come out of it, she was sure. Sam Clark's hold upon Neal would be shattered. They would go back to the Circle C, and Neal would be happier. She would be, too. She had never fitted socially in town, not with women like Mrs. Quinn and Mrs. Earl and the rest.

Pinning up her hair in front of the mirror, she wondered why Neal, in many ways a tough and unyielding man, had yielded to his father as much as he had. Habit, maybe. On occasion he had stood up to his father, but on the big things, like taking on the bank, he had submitted. Neal had a right to live his own life, she told herself defiantly. If it meant selling the bank, they'd do it.

She went down the stairs, determined to push Neal into the decision she knew he wanted to make. When she reached the parlor, she forgot all about it. Neal was dozing in a rocking chair, his pistol on his lap.

For a moment Jane stood motionlessly, vaguely alarmed. Neal should have been upstairs in bed. She walked across the room and shook him awake. He grunted and rubbed his eyes, then rose, and slipped the gun into his holster. He left the parlor and, crossing the dining room to the kitchen, closed the door after Jane who had followed him.

He grinned ruefully. "I sure turned out to be a good guard,

95

going to sleep like that. I'd get shot if I was in the Army."

She gripped his arms. "Neal, what happened? You've been up all night, sitting there with that gun on your lap. . . ."

"Wait'll I build a fire," he said. "I need some coffee."

She waited beside the stove until he had the fire going, the pine snapping with staccato cracks, then she set the coffee pot on the stove, and dropped into the chair Neal had placed there for her. He pulled up another chair and sat down, his angular face hard set, the muscles at the hinges of his jaws bulging like half marbles.

"What happened after you left the house last night?" Jane asked.

He hesitated, then told her about getting Joe Rolfe out of bed and going to Shelton's office and being shot at. "We still don't know whether those notes are bluffs, or whether Ed Shelly is alive and hiding around here."

"It's a trick," Jane said. "It's got to be. Joe has always told you Ed Shelly was dead."

"Sure, he's told me." Neal got up and walked to the window. "It's this thing about Laurie, Jane. If anything happens to her. . . ."

"It won't," Jane said. "We won't let it." She stared at his back, feeling the tension that was almost a physical sickness in him. "Neal, did you think they might be sending you those notes to keep you in the house? Darley and Shelton, I mean."

He turned sharply to face her. "And while I'm staying here, watching out for Laurie, they get out of town with the money. No, I hadn't thought of it." He frowned, and added thoughtfully: "And this is the day they have a man coming from Portland, a fat goose they aim to pick. It would work just as well for them if I stayed in the house as if I got out of town."

He would be safer here, she thought, but he would never forgive himself if he stayed at home, falling into the trap they were setting. No, he couldn't stay, built the way he was.

She said: "You go on to the bank. I'll take care of Laurie. I promise."

He looked at her doubtfully. "I don't know. This is Joe Rolfe's business. . . ."

"You've made it yours, darling. You can't hand it to Joe now." She rose and, going to him, put her hands on his shoulders. "Ed Shelly's been on your mind eight years, hasn't he?"

"How did you know?"

"You've talked in your sleep," she said. "You were dreaming about it, I guess. Sometimes it seemed as if you were having nightmares."

"I've had nightmares, all right," he said. "It was always the same whether it was you or Laurie or me who was being hurt. Ed Shelly had come back to Cascade City."

He whirled away from her and, going to the stove, poured himself a cup of coffee. "If Ed Shelly wanted to get square by worrying the hell out of me," he said, "he's getting it. Maybe I've worried so much about it, I brought it to pass." He tried to grin at her over the top of the coffee cup. "Fool notion, isn't it? I think I knew all the time I'd have to face something like this, but it's worse because of Laurie."

"Neal, maybe we're excited over nothing. They won't hurt Laurie if it is just a bluff. And even if Ed Shelly is hiding around town or out in the timber, he wouldn't take it out on Laurie. No man would."

"You're wrong," he said. "I've seen too many men do cruel things that were unreasonable. When I was a boy, a man who lived north of us beat his wife to death. And I knew a kid who skinned a cat while the cat was alive." He threw out his hands. "Don't ask me why men do things like that. Just something in them that makes them enjoy watching another person or an animal suffer."

"We'll be careful, Neal," she said. "That's all we can do. I'll get breakfast. . . ."

"No, this coffee's all I want." He turned toward the dining room door, then paused as he said: "I've got to see Laurie before I go."

Jane nodded, understanding, and followed him across the dining room and up the stairs to Laurie's room. She was awake, and, when she saw Neal, she jumped out of bed and ran to him, squealing: "I had the nicest dream, Daddy. I thought you were bringing a pony from the ranch for me to ride."

"I will, honey. I promise."

He caught her in his arms and held her high while she kicked and squealed, then he hugged her and her arms came around his neck and squeezed him hard.

"Dress me, Daddy," she said.

Jane stood in the doorway watching while Neal sat down on the edge of the bed and dressed her, his big fingers awkward with the little buttons on her dress. There was a lump in Jane's throat so big that it made her throat ache. This might be the last time Neal would ever dress Laurie. No, it couldn't be. She found herself thinking a prayer: *Don't let it happen, God. Don't let any harm come to either one of them.* She turned her back to them and wiped her eyes.

She heard Neal say: "I'll let Mamma put your shoes and stockings on. I've got to go to the bank. Laurie, your dream is going to come true. Not today, maybe, but real soon."

Jane turned around. She said: "Isn't that fine, Laurie?"

Laurie was staring at Neal, her eyes wide. "That little bay with the white stockings?"

"That's the one," Neal said. He picked her up and kissed her, then he whirled away and walked out of the room.

Jane said: "Let's get your shoes and stockings on. Then we'll go down and get breakfast." .

"What's the matter with Daddy's eyes?" Laurie asked. "He was blinking all the time?"

"I guess he had something in his eyes, honey. I've got a speck in mine, too." Jane finished buttoning the child's shoes and set her on the floor.

Laurie asked: "Can I go now?"

"Yes, you can go, but you'll have to stay in the house today."

"Why?"

"It isn't very warm outside and it's awfully windy. I don't want you to get a cold. Remember now."

"I'll remember," Laurie promised.

Jane left the room, walking fast and keeping her back to Laurie so the child wouldn't see the tears that were in her eyes again. *There is so much that is good in our lives, she thought, Neal's and mine and Laurie's. Why does it all have to be threatened now? Will we have to live with Ed Shelly's ghost the rest of our lives?*

CHAPTER TWELVE

Neal stepped out of the house into the morning sunlight that still held little warmth. He looked around, half expecting to see Shelton, or Darley, or Ruggles, but no one was in sight. He glanced at the threshold. No note this time. He closed the door and, crossing the yard, walked rapidly up the street toward the business block. Everything would come into focus today, he thought. It had to. He'd go crazy with the waiting if it didn't.

When he reached Main Street, he saw no one except the hardware man, Olly Earl, who passed without speaking. The irony of it struck him. He had been in Earl's store the day he'd shot the Shelly gang to pieces, but it didn't occur to the storekeeper that what was happening now might have its roots in that hold-up eight years ago.

Neal stepped into the Mercantile and, going to the post office that was located in a rear corner, opened his box. He took out a handful of mail: two papers, a bill, a catalogue, and one letter. He stared at the address—*NEAL CLARK, CASCADE CITY, OREGON*—written with a blunt pencil just as all the warning notes had been. He glanced at the postmark. The letter had been mailed here late yesterday.

"Harvey!" Neal shouted. "Harvey, where the hell are you?"

Quinn poked his head up from the counter on the other side of the room. "What's biting you?"

Neal crossed to the other side of the room and held out the envelope. "Got any idea when this was mailed, Harvey?"

Quinn was painting some empty shelves. Carefully he squeezed the brush against one side of the can and stood up. "How do you expect me to know when a letter's mailed?"

"I thought you might have noticed."

"Well, I didn't. Chances are it was mailed late yesterday afternoon. But, hell, you can't expect me to stand around and see who mails every letter. . . ."

"All right, Harvey, all right. Maybe you can remember whether Tuck Shelton or Ben Darley came in yesterday."

"Yeah. Shelton did. I sold him a box of Forty-Five shells."

"Did he mail anything?"

"I don't know, damn it." Quinn ran a hand through his hair. "What are you up to?"

"I've had some notes threatening my family. This looks like another one. I've got a hunch it's Shelton. Or maybe Darley."

"You're working damned hard to turn us against them," Quinn said. "I don't believe it. And I'll tell you something else. You keep fighting 'em like you have been, and you'll wind up on the end of a rope."

Here it was again. For a moment Neal stood staring at Quinn. He was a poor stick in many ways, the last man in town capable of intimidating anyone who had a spoonful of guts in his body. Middle-aged, thin, and crotchety, he was inclined to be overly cautious with his credit, but he was one of Neal's leading critics because the bank was careful with its credit.

There were several things Neal wanted to tell Quinn, but what was the use? Yesterday he had tangled with Alec Tuttle, and no good had come of that. No good would come from quarreling with Quinn, either, so he left the store and angled across the street to the bank.

As usual, Henry Abel was at his desk, working on a ledger. Neal wondered how many hours he spent each day in his swivel chair, bent forward, pen in his hand, the green eye shade on his forehead. But Abel was happy. Maybe he'd be happier yet if the bank were his sole responsibility.

"Good morning, Henry," Neal said.

"Good morning." Abel looked up, smiled, and went on working.

Neal walked past the cashier to his office and closed the door. He tossed the mail on his desk, then picked up the letter and tore it open. He was not surprised when he read:

I'll get your wife as well as your kid. It's too late now to save their lives. You should have thought of that eight years ago.

Ed Shelly

Neal threw it down and paced the length of the room and back. A feeling of unreality gripped him, as if this were a part of that old horrible nightmare he'd had so many times. Funny, he thought, how it struck him. It seemed to him he was a spectator, watching a series of plays, so many of them that the sharp edge of his feelings had been blunted.

He sat down at his desk, staring at the papers Abel had left here for him. He had letters to write, but he wouldn't do anything today. Maybe he never would again. Maybe he'd just go off and let Abel handle all of it. He was still sitting there when he heard a knock on the door and called: "Come in!"

Joe Rolfe stepped into the office. "How are you, Neal?" the old man asked, his wrinkled face shadowed by concern.

"You ought to know." Neal handed him the note. "Another one in the mail this morning. They're fools, Joe. You can make a man go crazy, but that's as far as you can make him go. What are they trying to do?"

Rolfe looked at the note and threw it on the desk. "You ain't quite crazy yet, Neal, and you ain't dead. They'll settle for either one. If you blow up when the stage gets in, there'll be a mob after you with a rope. That's why I'm here. You've got to stay in

102

the bank or go home."

"I won't do either," Neal said.

Rolfe sighed. "You're making a mistake, son. Jane and Laurie are more important to you than anything that can happen when the stage gets in."

Neal shook his head. "Jane's home. She can handle a gun, and she knows what's been going on. Now suppose you tell me what's so important about the stage getting in."

"Darley's spread the word about this fellow, Stacey. If he invests ten thousand dollars in the deal, Darley says they'll start work in the morning. Even if you get a report from your survey crew, it'll be too late if Stacey is the sucker Darley thinks he is."

"Stacey may be a ringer," Neal said. "Playing Darley's game. Thought of that?"

"Sure I've thought of it," Rolfe said, "but it don't make sense. They ain't got anything to gain by playing it that way because they've already milked this country for all it's worth, unless you make the loans they want. What I'm saying is that, if you jump in and tell Stacey what you think of the project, they'll lynch you. Tuttle and O'Hara and that bunch are like a wolf pack with Darley and Shelton running in the lead. This time I won't be able to stop 'em."

Neal got up and walked to the window. No one was in sight, but there was a long line of horses tied in front of O'Hara's bar. The farmers and townsmen were inside, drinking and listening to Darley. Rolfe was right. Anything could happen if Neal met the stage and tried to talk to Stacey. Rolfe was right, too, in saying the crowd would not believe the report of Neal's surveying crew if he had it. Too late, he thought bitterly, too late to do any good. Any good at all.

But he couldn't go home, and he couldn't just sit here in the bank when the stage wheeled in. Jane had said he had some of the flint that had been in his father. Maybe he had too much.

Maybe he was just mule-headed, but he had to stay here and try, and he had to depend on Jane to look after herself and Laurie. She could, he thought. She had the revolver and she'd keep the doors locked.

"I'm going to be on the street when the stage gets in," Neal said. "It's the only thing I can do and you know it."

Rolfe spread his hands. "Yeah, I reckon, seeing as you're Sam Clark's boy. There's another thing. This fellow, Ruggles, is in O'Hara's bar, but he ain't drinking much. He's talking about getting you."

"I sure won't stay off the street on his account." Neal wheeled from the window to face Rolfe. "Have you found out what the hook-up is between him and Darley and Shelton? I told you that when Missus Darley saw him yesterday, she got on her horse, and took off out of there like she had a bee under her tail."

"I don't know," Rolfe said. "I was in Shelton's office this morning. I gave him hell for shooting through the door, and he said just what Doc said he'd say . . . that he had to protect the money in their safe and he didn't know who was in the hall. I showed him them notes, but he didn't bat an eye. Claimed he'd never seen 'em. I mentioned Ruggles and he said he'd never heard of him."

"You didn't expect him to admit anything, did you?"

"No," Rolfe conceded, "but I figured I might be able to tell something from his face. Most men give themselves away when you get 'em in a tight corner, but not Shelton. You know, Neal, I have never seen that man show feeling of any kind since he came to town. Now I'm thinking he is about half cracked."

As Rolfe turned toward the door, Neal said: "It would take that kind of man to threaten a child."

"It sure would. Sometimes he acts like he's all frozen up inside." Rolfe opened the door and stood there, his hand on the knob, eyes pinned on Neal's face. "You won't change your mind?"

"No."

Rolfe sighed. "Well, I'll be on the street. So will Doc Santee. Maybe you'd better get Abel out there, too."

Neal shook his head. "Not Henry, Joe. He stopped a bullet once. I won't ask him to again."

"Yeah, reckon that's right. Well, you're a brave man, Neal, or a damn' fool. I ain't sure which."

Rolfe closed the door. Neal looked at his watch. Almost an hour before the stage got in, if it was on time. He lifted his gun from the holster and checked it carefully, wondering how fast Ruggles was. If he was Shelton's man, he must be good or Shelton wouldn't have hired him. This was probably Shelton's plan, to have Ruggles jump him and kill him before he had a chance to talk to Stacey.

Suddenly Neal was aware of voices in the bank, of Henry Abel saying: "Wait a minute. I'll see if he's busy."

And a woman screaming at him: "I don't care how busy he is! I've got to see him!"

The door flew open and Mrs. Darley rushed into the office. Henry Abel was ten feet behind her, red in the face with anger.

Abel shouted: "I told her to wait . . . !"

But Mrs. Darley was in no mood to wait for anybody. She took hold of the lapels of Neal's coat and twisted them in her hands, her upturned face very close to Neal's. He saw terror in her eyes, real terror. Her face was pale, her lips quivering. Suddenly he discovered she no longer held any appeal for him. She was just a frightened woman, a stranger, running to him for help.

"Neal, you've got to leave town. You've got to take me with you." Releasing her hold on his coat, she put her arms around his neck and tried to bring his lips down to hers, but she didn't succeed. She cried out: "What's the matter, darling?"

Behind her Henry Abel stood in the doorway, thoroughly shocked by this display.

CHAPTER THIRTEEN

For a horrible moment Neal looked past Fay Darley at Abel, afraid that Abel would tell his wife, and knowing what she would do with this if she heard. Then he jerked Mrs. Darley's arms away from his neck and roughly pushed her away.

Mrs. Darley whirled to face Abel, screaming at him: "This isn't any of your business!" She gave him a hard push, slammed the door, and turned back to Neal.

"You'd better leave," Neal said. "If you're trying to break up my home or fix it so I can't live in this country, you're going to get fooled. I happen to be in love with my wife."

"I don't care anything about your old home or your wife," she cried, "and you won't live anywhere if you don't get out of here! Can't you understand? I'm trying to save your life."

This was more of the same, he thought, anything to get him out of town. He said: "I never asked you for help and I never will." He motioned toward the door. "Now get along."

"I won't go. I'm in trouble and so are you. Ruggles was brought here by Shelton and Darley. He was hiding in the brush yesterday and he heard everything we said. He told Darley all about it. Darley was so mad I thought he was going to kill me this morning. Maybe he will yet. I'm scared, Neal. I was never so scared in my life."

Neal found it hard not to believe her. She showed her fear in her voice and her face. Either it was real or she was the greatest actress in the world. He asked: "You mean Darley's jealous?"

"No, no." She gestured impatiently. "He didn't want you to know Stacey was coming this morning. Or at least that ten thousand dollars was at stake. He's afraid you'll keep Stacey from investing in the project."

Half truth and half lie, he thought. *Just enough truth to sound good.* He said: "I don't believe you. It doesn't make sense that Ben Darley's wife would come here and talk to me like this unless he had his reasons for sending you."

"You fool," she said in exasperation. "What does it take to make you understand? They're afraid of what you'll do and say, so they're going to kill you. I don't know how. Maybe a lynch mob. Or Ruggles may force you into a fight. I tell you I don't know what they'll do, but I do know they aim to kill you."

"I'll take care of myself," Neal said.

"The hell you can," she flared. "Not against them. You're stubborn and you're stupid. They're playing for ten thousand dollars. They won't let you or me or anyone else keep them from getting it. When they do get it, they'll take it and all the rest of the money that's in the safe, and run."

He looked at her flushed face, almost compelled to believe she was telling the truth. But even if she was, he thought, she was still playing Darley's game. Maybe they did intend to kill him, but, on the other hand, it would be far cheaper and safer to get him to leave than to kill him.

"Go back to Darley and tell him it didn't work," Neal said.

"You crazy damned fool." Her hands knotted at her sides. "You can't get it through your head that you're up against killers. Murderers. Shelton hates you. He wants to see you dead. Darley's just greedy. He's not a killer like Shelton and Ruggles, but he could be and he would be for ten thousand dollars. Besides that, there's fifty thousand in the safe over there in the office. They planned this for months before they came here. Do you think for a minute they'd let your life or mine stand in their way of getting out of here with that money?"

"I may be stubborn and stupid," he said, "but I can't quit and run. Maybe you are in trouble because you talked too much to me, but you brought it on yourself. I can't help you." He walked to the door and put a hand on the knob. "Good day, Missus Darley."

"Wait, Neal!" she cried. "Don't open the door yet. There's another thing I haven't told you. I didn't want to because I wanted you to think well of me, but, if it will make you believe I'm trying to save your life, I'll tell you. I'm not Ben Darley's wife. He hired me to come here and pretend to be his wife."

Neal's hand dropped from the doorknob. "Why?"

"I'm not much good," she said miserably. "I'd do almost anything for money and I guess I have. I've been around men like Darley and Shelton all my life. You're different, Neal. I wasn't lying to you when I said I'd had my dreams about you. I wanted a decent man, and you are . . . so decent that you'd throw your life away because of something you believe to be your duty." She walked to him and gripped his arms. "I'd take you on any terms. I'd do anything you wanted me to do. Just go away with me. Now. Before it's too late."

"You didn't answer my question. Why did Darley hire you to be his wife?"

"He wanted a wife to help him appear respectable. He's worked these swindles in little communities like this before. He knows how these people think and feel. He said he wanted an attractive woman who could work in his office, but who would go with him to church, too, and to people's homes when he was invited. People like Olly Earl and Harvey Quinn. So I took his money and came here and moved into the boarding house with him. I've slept with him and acted like the loving wife and all the time I've hated him. I didn't think I could ever hate anybody like I have him. He's no good, and Shelton's worse."

109

He saw misery in her face, and regret and shame, and he knew beyond any doubt that she was telling the truth, but the truth didn't change anything as far as he was concerned.

"I'm sorry," he said gently, "but even if I wanted to go with you, I couldn't. If they kill me, I'll be killed, but I can't run."

Tears were in her eyes when she said: "I guess I knew all the time that's what you'd say. Well, I've known one decent man in my lifetime."

She stood on tiptoes and kissed him, then he stepped away from the door. She opened it and walked out, heels striking sharply against the floor. Neal watched her until she stepped into the street, then she disappeared in the direction of Darley and Shelton's office.

She could have told the truth, he thought, and still be doing exactly what Darley wanted her to do. It seemed to him that every move Darley and Shelton had made lately was prompted by the frantic desire to get him out of town before Stacey arrived.

Neal felt Abel's eyes on him. He turned to face the cashier. He said: "Henry, I may not live very long. If they get me, I expect you to stay with the bank."

"Of course I'll stay with the bank." Abel glanced at the street door, then brought his gaze back to Neal's face. His eyes were blinking constantly, the first indication that Neal had had of the tension that had seized the little man. He said: "Neal, don't go out there."

"I don t have much choice," Neal said.

"Yes, you do," Abel said. "If they kill you, they'll come after me. They'll force me to make the loans we've been refusing." He looked at the floor, licking his dry lips. "Neal, I suppose I'm a coward, but I almost died once right here in this bank. I don't want to go through it again."

Neal could understand that. He told Abel about the notes

he'd been receiving, then he said: "Maybe they don't have anything to do with Ed Shelly. If they don't, then Darley and Shelton must be the men who are responsible for me getting them. I've got to find out. Maybe I'll find out today." He nodded at the street door. "Out there."

Abel took a white handkerchief out of his pocket and wiped his face. He was afraid, almost panicky.

Funny how people fooled you, Neal thought. He had always considered Henry Abel a machine, born with a pen in his hand and the green eye shade on his forehead, a machine lacking the passions and fears that ordinary people had. With one exception. He was afraid of his wife.

"Maybe I won't throw my life away, Henry," Neal said, "but, whether I do or not, don't tell your wife or anyone what you saw, or what you're thinking about me and Fay Darley. In the first place, you'd be wrong. In the second place, you'd hurt Jane. And in the third place, you'd be doing exactly what they want you to do because they've been here long enough to know that your wife is the damnedest gossip in the county."

"I won't tell her. I won't tell her anything."

Neal returned to his office, having no confidence Abel could keep his word. But he had tried. It seemed to him that was all he was doing lately, just trying. He closed the door and stood at the window, staring at the crowd that was gathering on the other side of the street.

Good men, individually. He recognized most of them even at this distance. O'Hara, Sailor, Tuttle, Olly Earl, Harvey Quinn—men who had done business with Sam Clark for years. But Darley and Shelton were there, too, and they were the yeast that was making this human dough bubble.

Liquor, talk, greed, a sense of persecution slyly worked upon until it had become a savage feeling of being wronged—these were changing men from individuals into a mob. It would take only one act to bring it to fulfillment. The moment he tried to keep Stacey from investing in the irrigation project, they would be upon him, but that was the thing he must do.

Suppose he didn't say anything to Stacey? Darley and Shelton would get his $10,000 and they would probably leave the country within a matter of hours, taking the money that had been given to them by these very men who were standing in front of O'Hara's bar. Fay Darley had said that, which was exactly what Joe Rolfe had said all along they would do. For a moment he thought of asking Fay to tell publicly what she had told him, then decided against it. Even if she did, she wouldn't be believed.

The trouble was, as Joe Rolfe had said, he could do nothing until a crime had been committed. By the time this was known to be a crime, Darley and Shelton might be out of reach. If they succeeded, the county would be hurt, badly hurt, and the fine dreams Sam Clark had had would be set back a generation.

No, he couldn't let it happen. Even if he could get Stacey to postpone his decision until Neal had the report of the surveying crew, he would accomplish something. It was a matter of time. Sooner or later men like Darley and Shelton would be known for what they were.

He looked at his watch. Almost time for the stage. He checked his gun again. He thought of Laurie and Jane, of the ranch and the bank. If he died today, was Henry Abel man enough to do the job that would fall upon him? There was no way to know, but Neal thought he was.

Neal left the bank, his gun riding easily in his holster. He saw Doc Santee standing alone on the bank side of the street, and turned toward him. Neal had never seen the doctor wear a gun before, but he was wearing one today.

Santee grinned at him. "Almost time for the reception."

"I figured it was," Neal said.

Joe Rolfe was not in sight. Across the street the crowd was milling around in front of O'Hara's bar, impatient now. Shagnasty Bob, the driver, took pride in being on time. He was seldom more than a minute or two late in good weather, but he wasn't in sight yet.

Rolfe appeared, leaving the crowd to stride across the street to where Neal and Santee stood.

Santee said: "There's fifty of them, looks like, and three of us. You figure it's worth dying for, Joe?"

"Nobody's gonna die," Rolfe said. "Neal, go take that gun off."

"Are you crazy?" Santee demanded. "Trying to make a sitting duck out of him?"

"No, you know damned well I ain't," the old man snapped. "I've been talking to Darley. He says he don't have no objection if Stacey talks to Neal. But it's got to be inside the bank. If Neal jumps Stacey on the street, there'll be hell to pay, the crowd feeling the way it does."

Rolfe looked at Neal, waiting for him to say he'd wait.

Santee nodded as if he saw sense in what the sheriff said. "What about it, Neal?" Santee said. "You could wait inside the bank. We'll fetch Stacey."

Neal didn't answer. At that moment Ruggles shoved and elbowed his way through the crowd until he stood alone on the other side of the street, a bitter, vindictive man.

He called: "Clark? You hear me, Clark?"

"I ain't gonna stand for this," Rolfe said angrily. "I told that bastard not to make trouble."

Santee caught his arm. "You've lived too long in this country to think you can butt into a deal like this. They've got to have it out, after Ruggles said what he did."

"What did he say?" Neal asked.

"That he saw you and Missus Darley in the brush. . . ."

Neal stepped off the walk, not waiting for the rest. He called: "I hear you, Ruggles, and I want everybody else to hear! You're a liar, a god-damn' liar!"

The crowd parted behind Ruggles, leaving him alone as Neal was alone, in the morning sun, sharp and bright on the gray dust of the street.

CHAPTER FOURTEEN

Neal had seen men face each other with guns on their hips right here on this very street, never dreaming that someday he would be playing a part in the same grim drama. Cascade City was an island around which the current of civilization had flowed. It would change when the railroad came, but it had not changed yet. Here men still decided their personal differences with guns. Doc Santee understood this. So did Joe Rolfe.

This was not like the time Neal had shot the Shelly gang to pieces. That had been spontaneous, but this was deliberate, and Ruggles let it play out, hoping to break Neal's nerve. Suddenly— and he was surprised by it—Neal discovered he was not afraid. He didn't look around for Shelton or Darley; he kept his attention riveted on Ruggles, his right hand close to gun butt.

There was this moment that seemed to drag on and on. A wind raised a faint haze of dust, and from somewhere behind the Mercantile a dog barked, a sudden, disturbing sound in the silence. In the end it was Ruggles who broke, not Neal. He threw out a curse and went for his gun.

Ruggles was fast, recklessly and unbelievably fast, and that was his undoing. He squeezed off two shots before Neal fired; one bullet kicked up dust in front of Neal and to his right, the other came close enough to his head for him to hear it snap past. Then Neal's gun sounded, powder flame a quick burst of fire, the report hammering into the silence to be thrown back between the false fronts in slowly dying echoes.

Ruggles was knocked back and partly around as his finger jerked off a wild shot that was ten feet over Neal's head. Neal's second bullet put him down. His gun fell from slack fingers, his hat came off his head to topple over so it lay with the crown in the dust.

Joe Rolfe stepped into the street, his gun in his hand. "Don't make no fast moves. Hear me, Shelton?"

"I got nothing to do with this fight, Sheriff," Shelton said indignantly.

Neal ran to the fallen man, Doc Santee a step behind him. Neal knelt beside Ruggles, asking: "Who hired you to kill me?"

Blood bubbled on Ruggles's lips. He said: "I wasn't supposed to kill you. Just wound you so . . . you . . . couldn't . . . see . . . Stacey."

"Who hired you?" Neal demanded. "Who paid you?"

"Easy, boy," Santee said. "He's not going to answer any questions." Santee motioned to the men on the walk. "Earl. Tuttle. Give me a hand here. Let's get him off the street before the stage gets here." In a low tone, he said: "Get over there where you were. Watch it now."

Neal walked back to the other side of the street. He punched the two spent shells out of the cylinder and reloaded, then dropped the gun back into the holster. The reaction hit him and he began to tremble; sweat broke out all over him. He leaned against the front of the bank, his eyes closed. He was sick, he wanted to get back inside the bank, but he couldn't. They were watching him from the other side of the street, Darley and Shelton and the rest, hating him and now maybe fearing him a little. Joe Rolfe and Doc Santee had publicly sided him. That, too, might have a quieting effect if there was anything to this lynch talk.

He heard the stage, and someone yelled: "Here she comes!" The coach made the turn at the north end of the street, careening wildly for a moment before it settled down on all four wheels, dust piling up behind it in a stifling gray cloud. That was Shagnasty Bob's way, an old-time Jehu who used to make the run into Prineville from the Columbia before the railroad had been pushed south to Shaniko. He'd put on this same show as long as he was able to sit there on the high box and bring the stage roaring into Cascade City, or until the railroad came.

Neal wasn't sure which would end Shagnasty's career, old age or the railroad, but it was a good show, a relic out of the past just as the gunfight with Ruggles had been. Time would eventually put an end to both, and Cascade City would be tamed, but right now it was rough and wild and primitive. That was why men's tempers flamed high as they did, why lynch talk could be more than talk, even with Joe Rolfe wearing the star.

Ruggles's death had quieted the crowd for a time, but now the tension broke. Men ran into the street and formed two lines, yelling for Stacey and waving their hats. The stage wheeled between the lines, the silk flowed out over the horses to crack with the sharpness of a pistol shot. One moment the six horses were in motion, the stage rumbling and rattling behind them, then all motion stopped, and the street dust whirled up almost to hide horses and stage.

Shagnasty Bob, bearded and leather-faced with the front of his hat brim rolled up, yelled: "I fetched him, boys! It's up to you now. I done my part."

Darley opened the coach door and extended his hand. "This is a grand day for Cascade City, Mister Stacey. I'm Ben Darley."

"I'm glad to be here, Mister Darley," Stacey said as he stepped down. "When I return, if I'm still alive to return, I'm going to Shaniko by oxcart. I'll never trust my life to this wild man again."

Shagnasty Bob bellowed a great laugh and slapped a leg.

Dust boiled up from the blow. "I got you here, didn't I, Stacey? What more can you ask from a man?"

Shagnasty Bob had his moment and only one, then he was forgotten. The crowd surrounded Stacey as the stage wheeled away. They all had to shake hands with Stacey, from Shelton and Harvey Quinn and Olly Earl on down to Sorrenson, the livery stable kid. Then, studying the crowd, Neal suddenly realized that Jud Manion was not here and he wondered about it.

Aside from Manion, Henry Abel was probably the only man in the county who wasn't on hand to greet Stacey. He remained inside the bank. Joe Rolfe and Doc Santee waited with Neal in the fringe of the crowd, letting the others go ahead. Noticing this, Neal wondered what was in their minds.

From where he stood, Neal had a chance to study Stacey. The man was middle-aged with gray hair and mustache. He was small, but he moved with bird-like spryness that convinced Neal he was tougher physically than his size indicated. He was no fool, either. Neal was sure of that as he watched the man's animated face. He would listen, Neal thought, if they had a chance to talk.

Suddenly the handshaking stopped, and there was a moment of awkward silence as if nobody knew what the next move should be. Then Santee and Rolfe stepped up and introduced themselves. Santee said something, and Stacey nodded.

He said: "Sure, I want to meet your banker. If he wasn't here, I'd look him up."

"Hold on!" Tuttle bellowed. "He ain't no man for you to talk to, Mister Stacey."

And O'Hara: "He ain't for a fact, Mister Stacey. Let's step into my place and we'll have drinks all around on the house."

The crowd howled its pleasure and started toward O'Hara's bar, but Stacey didn't move with it. Darley and Shelton stood beside him, Darley showing his irritation, but, to Neal's surprise,

Shelton was affable enough as if this didn't cut any ice with him either way.

Neal moved toward Stacey, his hand extended. "I'm Clark, the banker. I want to talk to you, but I don't think the street's the right place. Why don't we step into the bank . . . ?"

"No," Darley interrupted. "Mister Stacey has had a long, hard ride. He's tired and he needs a drink."

"No hurry," Stacey said. "Is there some reason I shouldn't talk to Clark, Darley?"

"He thinks so," said Neal. He liked the way Stacey shook hands, the way his sharp eyes met Neal's. "You see, I'm opposed to this project. So are the sheriff and the doctor. I want to give our side of this business before you make any commitments."

Most of the men, realizing Stacey was not with them, turned in time to hear what Neal said. With Tuttle in the lead, they charged back. Rolfe stopped Tuttle by stepping in front of him, and Santee drove a shoulder into O'Hara and almost upset him.

Then Shelton, to Neal's surprise, called: "Let him talk, boys! Clark will hang himself if we give him enough rope."

"By God, we'll give him the rope!" Tuttle bawled.

The forward motion stopped, the angry voices subsided. Bewildered, Stacey said: "It strikes me there's more to this than mere opposition, Clark. Is it simply that you're taking a banker's natural stand against speculation?"

"It goes deeper than that." Neal nodded at Darley. "Will you come into the bank with us? I understand you told Joe you didn't object to me talking to Stacey?"

Red-faced, Darley said: "Later, Clark. I object strenuously to your talking to him the minute he gets to town."

"All right," Stacey said. "Clark, I'll drop over to the bank as soon as I cut the dust out of my throat."

"No, I'll have my say now," Neal said. "First, I want to assure you that we welcome men with capital. Someday Cascade City will be a big place. It needs your money the same as any undeveloped town needs capital. So does the county. As far as the people are concerned, you will never find better folks. I'm asking you to do just one thing, and I've got to say it before Darley talks to you."

"Not now," Darley said. "Mister Stacey, it's important that we don't waste any more time than. . . ."

"This is the damnedest thing I ever ran into," Stacey interrupted. "You've been here six months, Darley. You've been writing to me almost that long. What does a few minutes mean right now, one way or the other?"

"It means a lot," Darley said. "I promised the local men that, if you invest the amount we've been discussing by mail, we'll start work in the morning on the ditch. Clark here has done nothing but delay us from the day we came to town, and for no reason."

"I've had plenty of reason," Neal said. "Stacey, right now a survey crew that I hired is checking Darley and Shelton's proposed ditch line. I'll have a report in a day or two. All I want you to do is to wait until I get that report before you make any promises."

"Wait, wait, wait!" Darley screamed in a burst of infantile rage. "That's all we've done for weeks, Mister Stacey. Well, Shelton and I are done waiting. If the people of this community will do nothing but fight progress. . . ."

"Darley, I don't understand this need for haste," Stacey said sharply, "but, in any case, I refuse to be stampeded into anything. Who's making your survey, Clark?"

"Commager," Neal said. "From Prineville. Everybody in town knows him. Boys, I've got a proposition. If Commager's report is favorable, the bank will loan every one of you the amount you've been asking for. Don't tell me the company won't need it if Stacey comes in. I never saw an irrigation project in my life that didn't need more capital than the promoters thought when they started."

"It's a trick," Tuttle said sullenly. "You won't do it when the chips are down, Clark."

"Come over to the bank, Tuttle," Neal said. "We'll make out the papers this morning, with the proviso that the money be deposited to your account if and when we get a favorable report from Commager."

"That's fair," Stacey said. "I'm tired, Clark. I'll see you after I get a drink and something to eat."

"How about it, Tuttle?" Neal asked.

"I'll take your word for it," Tuttle muttered, and turned away.

Doc Santee caught up with Stacey. "You're having dinner with me as soon as we get that free drink O'Hara promised."

"It will be a pleasure," Stacey said, and turned his head to call back: "Darley, fetch my valise!"

Neal, glancing at Darley's face, saw the black fury that was in the man. Suddenly Darley stooped and picked up the valise and walked away. Neal looked at Shelton, realizing that those strange, opaque eyes had been pinned on him for some time. Shelton, he saw, showed no fury. Not even disappointment. But there was a strange attitude of eagerness about him as if he were waiting impatiently for something to happen.

It doesn't make any difference to him, Neal thought. *The money is all that matters to Darley, but Shelton's got something else on his mind.*

As Neal turned toward the bank, Rolfe caught up with him. "You stopped 'em dead, Neal. You sure did. I didn't know Commager was out there on the job."

"I figured it was a good idea to keep mum about it until I knew what his report was," Neal said, "but, when Stacey got here, I had to speak my piece."

"Everybody trusts Commager," Rolfe said. "If his report is what you think it'll be, you drove a nail right into the lid of Darley's coffin. That means they'll move out tonight with the money. If they do, I'll nab 'em."

"Holler if you need me," Neal said, and Rolfe nodded as he turned away.

Now, in this moment of quiet, Neal thought of Laurie and Jane. Wheeling, he started up the street toward home. They were all right. They had to be. Tuck Shelton and Ben Darley were here where they couldn't harm Laurie or Jane, and Ruggles was dead.

But Neal hadn't been home for several hours. He had to see Laurie and Jane again, had to know they were all right, and suddenly the dam of self-control broke and he began to run.

Chapter Fifteen

When Neal reached his house, he found the front door locked. He searched his pockets, but discovered he had left the key inside. He yanked the bell pull, momentarily irritated until he remembered that Jane was following his order. He jerked the bell pull again, the need to see Jane and Laurie a driving urgency in him.

Jane unlocked the door and opened it.

Neal demanded: "Are you and Laurie all right?"

"Of course," Jane answered. "Are you?"

"Sure," he said, trying to match her matter-of-fact tone.

Laurie heard him and ran out of the parlor, screaming: "Daddy, Daddy!" He scooped her up into his arms and hugged her so tightly she cried: "You're hurting me, Daddy!"

"I'm sorry," he said, and put her down.

She ran into the parlor, apparently thinking of something she wanted to do. She was always running, Neal thought, always in a hurry to get some place faster than she could by walking. She was usually excited about something, too, her voice made high by it. If anything happened to her so she couldn't run and couldn't squeal. . . . He looked at Jane and saw that she was close to crying. The same fear was in his wife's mind, he thought.

He walked into the parlor, ashamed of the emotion that suddenly made him weak. There was no reason to be, he thought. It was just that he had never been one to show his feelings, not even when he'd been a boy. He often wished he weren't the way

123

he was, that he could talk to Jane with the sweetness and tenderness he knew she needed, but it was hard for him. When he did, it was forced, lacking the spontaneity it should have had.

Laurie ran upstairs for something. Neal got out his handkerchief and blew his nose, his back to Jane. He couldn't remember feeling this way before, a dull ache in his chest and an all-gone emptiness in his belly. Reaction from killing Ruggles, he thought. Or from relief, knowing now that Laurie and Jane were all right.

Well, they were going to stay all right. He wouldn't leave the house until Darley and Shelton were in jail. They were whipped. He was sure of that. They'd make their run tonight and Rolfe would arrest them, and the greedy hardheads like Tuttle and Sailor and O'Hara would find out what Darley and Shelton had intended to do all the time.

"Neal."

He turned. Jane stood just inside the hall doorway. He saw that she had been crying, and he asked: "What's the matter?"

"You don't know?" she asked. "Neal, don't you know?"

She put her arms around him and he held her close. He touched her hair, saying as lightly as he could: "I don't have the foggiest notion. I'm the one who's been worrying."

She was angry then and stepped back, her face showing her resentment. "Don't you give me any credit for feelings? I heard those shots a while ago. I thought that Shelton and Darley were trying to kill you. Or that O'Hara and Quinn and Olly Earl. . . ."

"So you've heard that talk. Some of our gossipy neighbors. . . ." He stopped. No use to vent his anger on Jane. He moved to her and took her hands. "I'm sorry. I just haven't been thinking very straight lately. But it wasn't anything like that. It was this fellow Ruggles who's been hanging around. Shelton was behind it, I suppose. Anyhow, it didn't work. I got him."

Resentment fled from her face. "You mean he tried to kill you?"

"Yeah, he tried. It was just before the stage got in. I was standing in front of the bank, waiting like everybody else, and he comes out of O'Hara's bar and jumps me."

"Where was Joe Rolfe?"

"He was there."

"Couldn't he stop it?"

She should have known better than to ask a question like that. Short-tempered again, he said: "Joe didn't try."

She whirled, her skirt billowing out from her slim ankles. She said—"Oh, you men!"—and started toward the kitchen.

"Dinner ready?" he asked.

"No, it isn't," she flung over her shoulder, and disappeared into the dining room.

Neal rolled and lighted a cigarette, realizing he shouldn't be irritated, that he shouldn't have spoken so brusquely to Jane. It was only natural that her nerves should be frayed, just as his were.

He couldn't relax, even now that he was here in his own parlor, knowing that no harm had come to Laurie and Jane. He took a long pull on his cigarette and let the smoke out slowly, then dropped into a rocking chair, his legs stretched in front of him.

Laurie came downstairs and wandered aimlessly into the kitchen. Neal smoked another cigarette, restlessness gathering in him again. He wasn't sure he could stay here all afternoon. Maybe he didn't need to. Darley or Shelton wouldn't try anything during the day. Maybe they hadn't been sending the notes. It might have been Ruggles, and, if that was true, the danger to Jane and Laurie was past.

He heard Laurie's shrill voice begging her mother to let her go outside to play, and he heard Jane say in a cranky tone to quit asking. She had to stay inside. This trouble was costing all of them, he thought, and he had been stupid in not realizing that Jane was paying the same price he was.

He tossed his cigarette stub into the fireplace and walked into the kitchen. Laurie was sitting on a chair sulking, her feet kicking the legs. Neal said: "That's not a pretty face you've got today."

Laurie stuck out her tongue at him. Thoroughly exasperated, Jane went into the pantry and came back with a stick. "I haven't had to use this on you for quite a while, young lady, but. . . ."

"Wait." Neal put an arm in front of his wife. "Laurie, you go up to your room and don't come back until you've got a pretty face." He winked at Jane. "Like your mama's."

Laurie got up and left the kitchen. Not running this time, but trudging as if she were the most put-upon girl in town. Neither Neal nor Jane said anything until she was out of sight and they heard her on the stairs, then Jane said: "A pretty face like mama's! Now isn't that a great thing to tell your daughter?"

Neal laughed, a sudden breaking of the tension that had kept his nerves tied up for hours. He kissed Jane on the tip of her nose. "It's the prettiest face I ever saw. Now what about dinner?"

She laughed, too, a shaky laugh but still a laugh. "Thank you for the grand compliment. I'll get dinner started right away. I forgot you didn't have any breakfast." She went into the pantry, calling back: "Now I want to know what happened this morning! Everything. I'm getting tired of being treated like I was Laurie's age."

He told her, leaving out Fay Darley's visit and what Ruggles had said in O'Hara's bar. She'd hear someday, but maybe not until this was over.

When he was done, she said: "Then we still don't know who

sent the notes or shot at you or whether there really is an Ed Shelly."

"No, but it was probably Ruggles who shot at me. Maybe the whole thing was just to make me run, or stay here in the house. Anyhow, Joe will pick them up tonight."

She stood in front of the stove, looking at him. "You really think it's over?"

"It will be as soon as Darley and Shelton clean out their safe and leave town."

She shook her head. "I don't think so. We don't know who sent the notes or what the purpose behind them was. We can't draw a good breath until we know the answers to both questions."

He rose, the good feeling of relief gone that had been in him a short time. Jane was right. He walked back into the parlor, remembering how Shelton had acted this morning. A killer, Fay Darley had called him. A half-crazy one, too, if Neal's judgment of the man was correct. No, Jane was right. Nothing would be settled until Shelton and Darley were locked up in jail.

The doorbell startled him. He walked into the hall, drawing his gun before he opened the door. He was surprised to see Henry Abel standing there because it was two hours until closing time, and Abel wasn't a man to go off and leave the bank.

"Come in, Henry," Neal said. "I didn't expect. . . ."

"No, of course you wouldn't." Abel slipped in quickly as if afraid to remain outside. "I locked the bank up and put a sign outside that it would be closed until morning. Have you got a gun? Another one, I mean?"

Puzzled, Neal said: "You're not much of a hand with a gun."

"No, but I can try. I can't stay in the bank. Ed Shelly saw his father and brother shot in front of the bank, and, if he really is around here somewhere, he'll try again. I've got a hunch." He swallowed. "Now don't go off half-cocked. I'm saving you and me both a lot of trouble by locking the bank up in case O'Hara and Quinn and the rest of them get a notion they can force you to make the loans they want. The proposition is Darley doesn't want to wait for Commager's report."

Neal motioned for Abel to go into the parlor. "What do you want with a gun?"

"One gun isn't as good as two," Abel said as he walked into the parlor. "Three's still better. Jane shoots pretty well, doesn't she?"

"Yes, she's a good shot." Neal walked to the fireplace and leaned against the mantel, looking at Abel. The man was pale and trembling, thoroughly frightened, and Neal had no idea what had brought it on. "Henry, what's the matter?"

"Maybe nothing," Abel said, "but Stacey has talked to Joe Rolfe and Doc Santee, and he told Darley he wouldn't make any decision until he had that report you told him about." Abel swallowed. "Darley almost went crazy. He told O'Hara and Quinn and that whole bunch that you'd killed the project. They'll try to lynch you, Neal. They're blaming you for everything."

"You think they'll come up here?"

"Sure they will. I came here to help you fight."

Neal thought about it a minute, knowing that what Abel said was a definite possibility. Stacey's decision would bring this to a head, and with O'Hara setting up the drinks. . . . Neal rubbed his face, wondering how he could ever have felt they were out of the woods.

"There's a Thirty-Eight upstairs on the bureau," Neal said, "and a Twenty-Two pistol in the pantry. It's on the top shelf to keep it out of Laurie's reach. If they want a fight, Henry, they'll get it."

"Good," Abel said.

Jane came into the parlor. "Hello, Henry," she said. "I didn't know you were here. Dinner's ready. I'll put another plate on the table."

"I'm not hungry, Jane," Abel said. "I'll just have a cup of coffee."

"Whatever you say, but there's plenty." She called Laurie, who came down the stairs slowly, still sulking. "You hungry?"

"No," the child said, then she saw Abel and ran to him. "Henry, they won't let me go outside and play. You tell them it isn't too cold."

He picked her up and carried her into the dining room. "It's pretty cold, Laurie. I just came in. My teeth are chattering." He snapped his teeth together. "See?"

She giggled. "You're fooling."

"No, it's cold," Abel said.

He put her down and she crawled into her chair. "I'll eat," she said, "but I'm not hungry."

"All right," Jane said. "We don't care if you're hungry or not as long as you eat."

No one talked while they ate except Laurie who was over her sulks and chattered incessantly. They had barely finished when the doorbell rang.

Neal glanced at Abel as he rose. "I'll see who it is," he said, and left the kitchen, wondering if Abel's fears had been realized.

His gun was in his hand when he opened the door. Joe Rolfe stood there. Doc Santee was in the street forking his black gelding, his Winchester in the boot. The sheriff's horse stood beside the gelding.

Neal replaced his gun, relieved again, and he thought how often this had happened. Every time he had thought their trouble was over, he had soon found it wasn't.

"I didn't expect you," Neal said. "Henry came a while ago and said Darley was trying to work up a mob."

Rolfe's lined face was bitter. "He tried, and for about an hour I thought he'd make it, but there's a little horse sense left in people. Saddle Redman up, Neal. We ain't got much time. After Darley seen he'd lost out all around, he and Shelton cleaned the safe out and pulled out with the money."

"Then everybody knows?"

"Some of 'em do, and the rest will hear soon enough."

Abel had followed Neal and had heard. He said: "Neal, let me ride Jane's mare. I'll go with you."

"No, you stay here with Jane and Laurie," Rolfe said. "I ain't real sure what happened, not sure enough to leave Neal's womenfolk alone in the house. I'm glad you're here, Henry."

"If there's any chance those bastards are still in town," Neal said, "I'm not going."

Rolfe jerked his head at Neal. "Come on, I'll help you saddle up."

They walked around the house to the barn, Neal saying stubbornly: "Joe, I've been through hell worrying about what was going to happen to my family. I tell you. . . ."

"They ain't around," Rolfe broke in. "I didn't want Henry going with us. I found out years ago that a small posse of men I can count on is a hell of a lot better'n a big one of men I ain't sure about. I ain't sure about Henry. Sometimes I think he ain't got no guts at all."

"He doesn't have as far as his wife's concerned," Neal said, "but I think he'd be all right on something like this."

"Well, he's not used to riding," Rolfe said. "He's better off here. Go ahead and saddle your horse and I'll tell you what happened. It's like I said this morning. I figured they'd make their run tonight, so I wasn't paying no attention to 'em. Fact is, I didn't even know they'd left town until Jud Manion rode in a while ago. He'd been over to Prineville trying to borrow some money, and he seen Darley and Shelton riding toward the desert, hell for leather. Jud started toward 'em, and one of 'em took a shot at him. He got sore, as any man would, so he told me soon as he got to town."

Embarrassed, Rolfe cleared his throat. "I should have been watching, but I wasn't. I hiked up to their office, and, by God, that safe was open and clean as a hound's tooth. Nobody there. When I started asking questions, nobody had even seen 'em lately."

"Stacey?"

"Stacey hadn't, neither. I went to the livery stable. Shelton had taken their horses, saying they was heading out to Barney Lakes to see your survey crew. It would have made sense if I hadn't seen the empty safe."

"We'll find the money on them, won't we?" Neal asked, leading Redman out of the barn. "They wouldn't be likely to cache it, and come later?"

"No, sir," Rolfe said. "This is a place they won't ever want to come back to. Better put your sheepskin on. It's gonna get mighty cold if we don't catch up with 'em before sundown."

Rolfe took the reins and led the horse around the house. Neal went inside, told Jane what had happened, and kissed her and Laurie. He came out a moment later, wearing his sheepskin and carrying his rifle. Henry Abel was waiting with Rolfe and Doc Santee.

"Stay here, will you, Henry?" Neal asked. "I don't think there's any trick to this, but I'd feel better if I know you're in the house."

"Sure, I'll stay," Abel said, nodding gravely.

Neal mounted and rode east, Rolfe on one side of him, Doc Santee on the other. Once he looked back to wave. Jane and Laurie were on the front porch with Abel. All three waved, then Neal turned and did not look back again.

Jud Manion understood at last, Neal thought. So would the

others, but Manion was the one whose friendship he had hated most to lose. But as he thought about it, it struck him there was something which wasn't quite in place, some little part that didn't fit.

Then it came to him. He asked: "Joe, where's Missus Darley?"

"Hell, I don't know. She wasn't in their office. I suppose she's at the boarding house."

She could be, Neal thought, but he remembered how close to panic she had been that morning, certain that her life was in danger. Then the terrifying thought came to him that Darley or Shelton might have killed her to keep her from talking. They were capable of it, and he didn't doubt that they would if they knew what she had told him this morning.

He was having his nightmare again, he thought. No, this was real. He could not shake the feeling that Fay Darley had been honest with him and somehow he was responsible for what had happened to her. He tried to put it out of his mind, but the doubt grew until it became a torturing sense of guilt.

CHAPTER SIXTEEN

Watching Neal ride away, Henry Abel wondered if it was over at last. He had seen the worry and tension grow steadily in Neal, and now if he could relax. . . . But he couldn't because it wasn't over and it wouldn't be over until Darley and Shelton were in jail or dead, and Neal knew for sure who had written the notes and what the intention was behind them.

I should have gone and let Neal stay here, Abel thought. He started to say that, then held his tongue as Laurie went skipping past him and through the door, calling something to her mother.

"We've still got to be careful," he said. "I'm going to stay here till Neal gets back."

But worry had rolled off Jane's shoulders. She laughed and shook her head at him. "There's no need to, Henry. You go on home."

"To what?" he asked somberly.

Jane understood. "I'll be glad to have you, if you want to stay. I just don't think it's necessary."

She went into the house, but he stood outside for several minutes, unable to feel the confidence Jane did. He was haunted by a vague worry he could not identify except that it seemed to him danger had disappeared too quickly to be real. But maybe he had overestimated the danger, maybe he listened too much to the idle talk of men like O'Hara and Quinn and Olly Earl when the only real danger had been from Darley and Shelton,

133

and perhaps from Darley's wife. She was a bitch if he'd ever seen one.

The uneasiness lingered in him even after he went back into the house. He stood in the parlor, listening to Jane and Laurie's chatter from the kitchen. They were too far away for him to hear what they said, but it wasn't important. He thought about Neal and Jane and Laurie, and about his own wife, who he was sure he hated. He shook his head. He wasn't going to think about her now. This was important. He could think about his wife any time.

A moment later Jane went upstairs with Laurie, and, when she came down, she said: "Laurie's taking her nap. I'm going downtown if you're going to stay here. I haven't been out of the house all day."

"I'm staying," Abel said stubbornly, sensing that Jane didn't really want him to stay. She didn't have any confidence in him for a thing like this. Joe Rolfe didn't, either. Well, by God, he'd show them. He said roughly: "Jane, Neal said he left a Thirty-Eight revolver on the bureau upstairs. Will you get it for me?"

She hesitated, then said—"All right."—and went upstairs to her bedroom, returning a moment later with the gun. She handed it to him and went on to the hall door. "I won't be gone long." Then she turned and looked at him. "Henry, you don't think Neal will get hurt?"

"No, there's three of them. Shelton's the one they've got to look out for. Darley's just got a slick tongue."

"I guess they won't be back for a long time."

"May be quite a while," he said, "but Joe Rolfe knows the high desert like you know your front yard. So does Neal."

She laughed shakily. "Funny how I felt a while ago. Like I'd been all bound up. Tied so I couldn't move or even breathe. Then when I heard that Darley and Shelton had left town, it seemed like we were free. Like it was all over. But it isn't for

Neal. I guess I'm just selfish, thinking of myself that way."

"No, you aren't selfish," Abel said gently. "Neal's a very lucky man."

"Oh, I'm the lucky one, Henry. Well, I'll be right back."

He stood at the window watching while she went down the street, walking fast the way she liked to when Laurie wasn't with her. He'd seen her walking that way along Main Street, or stopping to talk with some other woman in town, her face animated. Neal was lucky, all right. He didn't know what a bad marriage was, or what it did to a man.

A knock on the back door broke into his thoughts. He crossed the dining room and went into the kitchen, his mind still on Jane. He opened the back door and froze, shocked into immobility. Tuck Shelton stood a step away, a gun in his hand. Ordinarily Shelton's face was devoid of expression, but now it was filled with a kind of wolfish eagerness.

So it had been a trick! Somehow Shelton and Darley had circled back to town.

Darley must be around here, too. Maybe in front of the house. Abel knew he had to do something. Shelton was alone now. If Abel had any chance, it would be before Darley and Shelton got together.

Abel had been a coward from the day big Buck Shelly had shot him, but he wasn't a coward now. He thought of Laurie upstairs, and of the notes Neal had received. He stood there, staring at Shelton for a matter of seconds, his thoughts racing. The man wouldn't shoot because he'd alarm the town.

Encouraged by that thought, Abel jumped back and grabbed for the .38 he had slipped under his waistband. But he was slow. Far too slow. Shelton took one quick step forward and slashed him across the head with the barrel of his gun. Abel went down in a loose-jointed fall, knocked cold.

Shelton holstered his gun. Picking up the .38 that Abel had

dropped, he looked at it, then stuck it under his waistband. He stood motionlessly for a time, his head canted to one side, listening, but he heard nothing. He shut the back door and quickly searched every room on the first floor. Finding no one there, he picked Abel up and carried him into the parlor and slammed him down on the couch.

He scratched his jaw thoughtfully, then swung around and ran up the stairs. He looked into the bathroom. Empty. So were the first two bedrooms, but the third wasn't. Laurie was asleep on the bed.

He retreated into the hall and shut the door. He grinned as he went down the stairs. Abel was beginning to stir. Shelton rolled him onto the floor and dug his toe into his ribs. He sat down on the couch, his revolver in his hand, and waited until Abel sat up, holding his head.

"Got a headache, banker?" Shelton asked.

Abel pulled himself into a chair and sat there holding his head.

Shelton said: "Better answer me."

"Yeah, I got a headache."

"Where's Clark?"

"Out in the desert with Rolfe and Santee. They're chasing you."

"Not me," Shelton said. "This didn't work quite the way I planned, but it's all right. I hid in a closet in the office and left the safe open. Rolfe took one look, and, when he saw the safe was empty, he lit out of there like his tail was on fire."

"Jud Manion told Rolfe he saw you and Darley."

"He saw Darley, all right, but not me. The other one was Fay, riding astraddle. Manion must have seen 'em off a piece and mistook her for me." He scratched his jaw, his opaque eyes narrowed. Finally he said: "Where I missed out was thinking Clark would stay home."

"I wish he had," Abel said. "You wouldn't be sitting there. . . ."

"Where's Missus Clark?"

"She went downtown."

"When will she be back?"

"I don't know."

Shelton was silent for several minutes, then he said: "You kind of like the Clarks, don't you, banker? You like 'em extra well, seeing as Clark's your boss."

"Sure I like them."

"Now that little girl sleeping upstairs. Be a shame if anything happened to her, wouldn't it?"

"If you touch her. . . ."

"Shut up, banker. You won't do anything if I touch her. You'd better keep hoping she don't wake up and start to bawl." He jabbed a forefinger in Abel's direction. "I don't like squalling brats. If she starts yelling, you'd better get upstairs and see she shuts up. If she don't, she gets hurt. And if you try leaving the house, or try anything when Missus Clark comes in, you'll get hurt. Savvy that?"

Abel nodded, his head hurting so much he couldn't think straight. He only knew that being shot eight years ago was nothing compared to the trouble he was in now. And there wasn't anything he could do about it. Not a damned thing.

Shelton sat on the couch ten feet in front of him, his gun on his lap, a grin on his wild, wolfish face. *He's just waiting for me to make a wrong move,* Abel thought, *but I won't do it. I won't do it.*

CHAPTER SEVENTEEN

Neal rode in silence when they left town. He had no desire to talk. Apparently Joe Rolfe and Doc Santee didn't, either. They probably felt as he did, a little limp now that it was practically over. It was simply a matter of staying on the trail of the two men until they were found. After all the uncertainty he had been through lately, Neal was sure of one thing. This would prove to everyone in the county that he had been right. The money would be on Ben Darley and Tuck Shelton.

Well, Rolfe would bring in the two men. They'd be jailed and tried and convicted and sent to the state prison at Salem, and that would be the end of the whole business. The money would be returned. No one, unless it was Fay Darley, would be badly hurt except for the broken dreams of greedy men. There would be no quick profits. O'Hara and Quinn and Tuttle and the rest of them would learn again that hard work and patience marked the slow passage to prosperity.

As Neal's father had said repeatedly, the exceptions are few indeed. But there were other dreams, the solid kind that his father had had that were far more practical than this will-o'-the-wisp thing Darley and Shelton had come up with. Holding back more water on the upper river so there would never be a shortage, a railroad giving downgrade passage to the Columbia, modern sawmills to harvest the pine crop that was ready for the harvesting—these were dreams worth working for and could be attained, with sweat and outside capital. Maybe he could get

Stacey interested before he went back to Portland.

Now, with the town well behind them, the narrow road cut eastward through solid walls of juniper; hoofs stirred the deep lava dust. Above them the sun dropped steadily toward the towering peaks of the Cascades, then the junipers began to thin until there was only a scattering of them in the sagebrush and lava ridges that were scabs in the shifting, sandy soil. They reached Horse Ridge and began to climb the road that was hardly more than a trail looping up the slope in long, sharp-turning switchbacks.

Neal had tried not to think about Fay Darley; he tried to keep his mind on the one important fact that the two men who had come close to bringing disaster to Cascade County were ahead. But now, with the sun almost down, he began to worry again. The uneasiness that had been in him when he'd left town had never completely deserted him.

He began thinking of the things that could go wrong. They might not be able to pick up the fugitives' trail. Both men knew the high desert. At least they had spent a good deal of time at the lakes in the Barney Mountain area. So, knowing the country, they could have taken any of a dozen routes.

If Darley and Shelton did escape with the money, the county's progress would be retarded for years. With typical human forgetfulness, the men who had invested in the project would blame Joe Rolfe and Neal for letting it happen.

"You figured it would go like this," Quinn or O'Hara or Tuttle would say, "and you let 'em get clean away. What kind of a law-man are you, Joe?" Or: "You wanted 'em to pull this off, Clark. You had to prove you were right."

Or it might have been a trick to get Neal and the sheriff out of town. Jud Manion would not have willingly had any part in such a maneuver, but he might have been used. Possibly they had shot at him so he'd do the very thing he had done. Darley and Shelton might have disappeared into the junipers and be headed back to town right now.

Neal could not stand it any longer. When they reined their horses to a stop halfway up Horse Ridge, he demanded: "How are you going to know which way to go, Joe? This is a hell of a big country."

Doc Santee was looking at Rolfe, too. The same question was in his mind, Neal thought. He had been called out here more than once to tend to a buckaroo with a broken leg or bullet hole in his belly. Invariably he'd ridden back to town alone, guided only by the stars. Like Neal, he knew how it was out here: dry washes, miles of rimrock that looked alike, alkali flats, and a juniper forest that ran for miles and miles, the trees so close together in some places that the only direction a man could see was up, a country where fifty men could lose themselves as easily as two.

Rolfe knew all of this as well as Neal or Santee did, and the doubts showed on his weather-burned face. He said testily: "I can guess what you're thinking. We're too far behind 'em to catch up. We didn't fetch any grub, and there's no place out here to stock up until we get to Commager's camp on the lakes."

"That's part of it," Neal said, "but there is a chance they might have circled back. We haven't been watching for any sign. Chances are we wouldn't have caught it anyway, with as many tracks out here on the road as there are."

Rolfe snorted his contempt. "They're ahead of us. You can count on it. Besides, why would they circle and head back, now that they've got the *dinero?*"

"Those notes I got were plenty of reason," Neal said. "You forget them?"

"No, I ain't forgot 'em," Rolfe snapped. "I thought about leaving you in town, and I would have if there was anybody else

I could have brought, but I didn't figure you'd get boogery like this."

"You still haven't explained those notes," Santee said.

Rolfe's frayed temper suddenly snapped. "Why, God damn both of you for a pair of chuckle-headed idiots. You know as much about this business as I do and most of the time you ain't stupid. They wanted Neal out of town and they had good reason. If he hadn't talked to Stacey when he did, everything would have been different."

Neal was silent. Whatever he said would be the wrong thing, with Rolfe as sour-tempered as he was. If Jud Manion had said he'd seen three riders, Neal would have been convinced that everything was just as it appeared to be. He didn't want to think they had killed her, but they wouldn't have gone off and left her, knowing she would talk. Darley might have dreamed up some excuse for being out here, but he wouldn't have any chance to make it stick with Fay testifying against him. Neal didn't know what to think, so the uneasiness continued to plague him.

Santee, too, said nothing. Presently Rolfe, a little ashamed of his outburst, said mildly: "If we'd hung around town long enough to get rigged out proper like, it would've been dark afore we got started. This way there's a chance we might catch 'em. Darley ain't no horsebacker." He cocked his head, glancing at the sun that was resting atop the peaks. "Gonna be dark purty soon. Maybe they'll stop and cook supper and we'll see the fire."

"Not Shelton," Doc said. "He's too old a hand at this game, if I've got him figured right."

Rolfe shrugged and started toward the top, with Neal riding beside him. Presently the sheriff said: "I've been digging at this in my head ever since we left town. Before that, too. Only one thing you can be sure of. Them notes you got was just a bluff to get you out of town so they could suck Stacey into the deal. I kept thinking Shelton had something else in his noggin, but I reckon he didn't."

Neal, remembering the fury he had seen so plainly in Darley when Stacey had arrived, and the unexplainable lack of anger in Shelton, was not convinced Shelton didn't have something else in mind. Suddenly he knew he had to go back. But he hesitated, not knowing how he could tell Rolfe about the crazy, twisting fear that was in him.

Santee said: "You ducked Neal's question, Joe. You're an old hand at this game, but being an old hand doesn't cut down the size of the country."

"I thought you'd forget the question, if I got you sidetracked," Rolfe said. "All right, I'll tell you the way I've got it figured. Darley's a weak sister. He'll break. The desert will do that every time to a man who ain't used to it. You both know that."

"Sure," Santee agreed, "but meanwhile we're riding. . . ."

"We'll head for the lakes if we don't pick 'em up between here and there," Rolfe cut in. "It's my guess we'll be hunting one man, not two. Shelton will plug Darley and go on with the dinero. I thought we'd get Commager and his men to help. Chances are we'll have to keep right on going. . . ."

A rifle cracked ahead of them; the bullet sounded to Neal as if it had barely missed him. He dug his spurs into Redman, swinging off the trail to the left; Rolfe and Santee went to the right. Again the rifle sounded, the bullet clipping a branch off a juniper tree just above Neal's head. Then he was behind a tall lava upthrust and pulled his horse to a stop. Jerking the Winchester from the boot, he swung down.

They had almost reached the top. Probably Shelton and Darley were forted up in a nest of boulders right on the rim. To go on straight up the ridge was sheer suicide. Again the Winchester cracked, the bullet striking the lava and screaming as it fled into space. Just one rifle. Neal puzzled over that. If Shelton and Darley were both here, there would be two. Darley might be a weak sister just as Rolfe thought, but he'd fight, cornered as he was.

One thing was sure. Neal couldn't go back now. Maybe Rolfe had been right in thinking Shelton would kill Darley and go on with the money. That could explain why only one rifle was working. But it didn't seem right. Shelton wasn't the kind to hole up. He'd be riding, and riding fast. He was too smart to stop and fight unless he had to, with the odds three to one.

Neal took off his hat and, breaking a branch from a deadfall juniper, poked his hat above the rock. The rifle shot came the instant the hat appeared. Neal pulled it down. No hole. It wasn't Shelton. He wouldn't have fallen for an old trick like that, or, if he had, he'd have hit the hat right through the band.

Neal's first reaction was one of relief. Darley must have shot Shelton. That meant Darley was outnumbered three to one. They should have no great difficulty getting him into a squeeze of some kind.

Neal looked across the road, but neither Santee nor the sheriff was in sight. The junipers were small and scattered here, but the lava that had spewed out of some ancient nearby crater was a tumbled mass clear to the top of the ridge. Darley had Neal pinned down, but there was a good chance Rolfe and Santee were working their way toward the rim, their horses hidden among the rocks.

The relief was short-lived in Neal. Shelton might have gone back. It was inconceivable that Darley could have got the drop on a man like Shelton and killed him. Neal remembered how he had quit fighting and crawled under the desk. No, Ben Darley was not a fighting man, and it would take a good fighting man to get the best of Shelton.

The need to find out what had happened to Shelton became

a necessity to Neal. He shouted: "Darley! Can you hear me, Darley?"

"Sure, I can hear you!" Darley called back. "You coming up to get me?"

"Where's Shelton?"

Darley laughed. "What will you give me to tell you?"

"Your life," Neal said, "if you'll throw out your gun."

Silence then. After what seemed minutes, Darley said: "He didn't leave town with me. He was going to call on your family. You know what he said in those notes."

It could be true. Or it could be a trick to get him into the open. Neal pulled his Colt, leaving the rifle leaning against the lava. He had to know.

Santee called from the other side of the road: "Stay where you are, Neal!"

But he couldn't stay. Time had run out for him. He lunged from the rock and started up the slope, slipping and sliding in the loose sand. Darley opened up the instant Neal came into view, bullets kicking up the dirt at his feet. At that moment, with lead striking all around him, the nearest rock that was big enough to give protection seemed a mile away.

CHAPTER EIGHTEEN

For a long time Henry Abel sat staring at Shelton, the throbbing in his head a constant ache. He had been afraid of many things in his life, but he had never experienced the hopeless fear he felt now. He knew that Neal was not immune to fear, but Neal was different. Abel respected him as he had never respected another man, and that was probably the reason. Neal conquered his fear, he did what he thought was right, and in that regard, Abel knew, Neal was a better man than his father had ever been.

Now, right now, Henry Abel knew he was up against something that would test him as he had never been tested. But what could he do? Jane would come in through the front door any minute. Laurie might wake up and start to cry. And Neal might not be home any time tonight. Maybe not even tomorrow.

Finally, because Abel could no longer stand the silence, he asked: "What do you want with Neal?"

"I'm going to kill him."

Abel shut his eyes. Shelton had said it as calmly as if it were something he did every day. A conversation like this couldn't be real. Abel was having a nightmare. But, when he opened his eyes, he knew it was no nightmare. Tuck Shelton hadn't moved. He might have been a figure carved of granite if it hadn't been for the blinking of his eyes, and that crazy, eager expression on his face.

Bitter self-condemnation was in Abel. He remembered his feeling that the trouble was over too quickly, too easily. He should have known, should have been more careful when he'd heard the knock on the back door. Now he and all the Clarks might die because of that one moment of carelessness.

He leaned forward, his hands pressed palm down against the couch on both sides of him. He asked: "Why do you want to kill Neal?"

"You can call it an old debt," Shelton said. "But maybe I won't kill him after all. Maybe I'll kill his wife or his kid and let him watch. I'm in no hurry to get it finished. But whatever I decide to do, he's going to watch."

Still no change in his expression. Abel forgot his headache. He even forgot how afraid he was. There was something strange about Shelton, something weird and unreal as if he had only one strong feeling of any kind that was driving him to murder. But why?

Perhaps he would never know, Abel thought. He could read nothing in Shelton's face except that crazy eagerness, an eagerness that, oddly enough, was balanced by the ability to wait. Watching Shelton, the thought occurred to Abel that the man actually enjoyed the waiting.

Neal might find out what was prompting Shelton to do this, after it was too late. There was no way Abel could warn him unless he was willing to sacrifice his own life. Abel wasn't sure what he would do when the time came. It all depended on what happened when Neal got here. He might walk into the house and be under Shelton's gun before Abel had a chance to do anything.

On impulse Abel rose, wondering what Shelton would do. He had to test himself, too, as well as Shelton's reaction. He hadn't moved for so long that he wondered if he were paralyzed. Fear could do that, he'd heard Doc Santee say.

146

Abel discovered he could move all right, up slowly and down rapidly. Shelton simply tilted the gun up so it was lined on his chest.

"You start getting boogery, and I'll blow your heart right out through your backbone," Shelton said. "Don't expect me to tell you again."

Abel licked his lips. He said: "Shelton, Laurie's alone. When she wakes up, she might be scared and start crying."

"I've already told you," Shelton said. "I can't stand bawling kids, so she'd better not start."

"Be reasonable!" Abel cried. "You can't keep a child of that age quiet."

"I can," Shelton said. "I can fix it so she'll be quiet for a long time."

He could and would, Abel thought. It was all right to tell yourself that a grown man would not harm a child like Laurie, but you'd be wrong because what an ordinary man would do had no relationship with what Tuck Shelton would do. So Abel sat, staring at the man, his head hammering, his mind reaching for something he could do, and finding nothing.

The front door opened. Abel started to get up again, and stopped when Shelton said: "Hold it, banker. Let's see who it is."

Jane, Abel thought. *It has to be her.* Again he had the terrifying thought that it might be days before Neal got back. What would they do? Jane? Laurie? What would he do? What could anyone do living in the house with a maniac. Abel would be driven out of his mind with fear and anxiety and the sheer tension of waiting. So would Jane. He didn't know much about children, but he did know that Laurie, used to running and singing and banging around the way she always did, could not be expected to remain quiet for any length of time.

But this was now, right now, with Jane coming in and not

knowing what she was going to find. Instinctively Abel sensed that the one thing they must do was to keep from shocking Shelton, to refrain from doing anything violent or sudden that would precipitate action. So, in spite of Shelton's warning to hold it, Abel said in a low tone: "Easy, Jane. Don't scream."

She stood in the hall doorway, head tilted back, mouth open, staring at Shelton, who had moved to one side of Abel so that he could shoot either Jane or Abel if he had an excuse. Jane might have screamed if Abel hadn't spoken the warning. As it was, she controlled herself, standing motionlessly, a basket of groceries in her right hand, a package of meat in the other. Her face turned pale, but she made no sound, and Abel felt a quick burst of admiration for her. Under these circumstances, his wife would have been hysterical.

"Good," Shelton said. "I was afraid you were going to start yelling. I can't stand yelling women. Crying ones, either. Fact is, I can't stand women unless they're good cooks. Can you cook?"

Jane nodded.

Abel said: "I've eaten here. She's a fine cook. It's time for supper. Why don't you let her show you?"

"I was thinking it was a good idea," Shelton said. "You cook a good meal." He nodded at Abel. "She'll need some wood, chances are. Fetch in enough for breakfast while you're at it."

Abel had not expected this. He got up and started toward the kitchen, fighting the temptation to run. Jane moved after him stiffly, as if she had lost control of her joints. Just as they reached the dining room door, Shelton said: "Wait."

They turned, Abel groaning in spite of his effort not to. Shelton had almost made a mistake. Once Abel was through the back door, he'd have headed for the alley and run for help. He'd have been back with someone in a matter of minutes.

But Shelton had not come as close to making a mistake as Abel had thought. He said: "Missus Clark, your daughter is upstairs asleep. I don't want to harm her. Not yet, anyhow. I don't want to do anything until your husband gets back. No sense in doing what I'm going to do unless he's here to see it. I've waited eight years. I can wait a few more hours."

He grinned at them. Not really a grin, Abel thought. More of a grimace, but it was meant for a grin. Shelton said: "I sent them notes to worry him. I did, didn't I?"

Jane was unable to say anything, so Abel said: "You worried him plenty."

"A small payment on what he owes me," Shelton said. "I'll collect the rest when he gets here. Trouble is, we don't know when that will be, do we?"

"No," Abel said.

"We may have to live together for quite a spell," Shelton went on. "Too bad you got caught here. Your wife's going to miss you, ain't she, banker?"

"She may start out looking for me," Abel said.

"But maybe she won't think of coming here," Shelton said. "I don't want anybody else in the house. If she does, get rid of her. And if you have any visitors, Missus Clark, get rid of them. Tell 'em Laurie's sick or something. She's got to stay in her room."

Shelton glanced at the stairs thoughtfully. "When she wakes up, you go tell her she's got to stay in her room and keep still. I was telling the banker I can't stand bawling brats. Now I'll tell you how it's going to be. My plan worked out perfectly except for one thing. I didn't figure on Clark leaving the house like he done. Well, nothing I can do now but wait for him. Until he gets back, you'll feed me. I'll sleep upstairs across the hall from your kid. I'm a light sleeper. If I hear anything wrong, I'll be into her room mighty damned quick. You know what I'll do to her?"

Jane nodded.

"What?" Shelton said. "You tell me, Missus Clark."

Jane moistened her lips with the tip of her tongue. She opened her mouth and shut it without saying a word, then swallowed.

"Well?" Shelton said. "Can't you talk?"

"You'll kill her," Jane whispered.

"That's right," Shelton said. "I don't want to yet, but I will if either one of you don't toe the line. I won't kill her quick, Missus Clark. Remember that, too."

Jane nodded again.

Abel simply stared at Shelton, knowing what was in his mind. Here was an animal-like cunning and cruelty that prompts a cat to promise freedom to a captive bird without having the slightest intention of keeping that promise. Still he had to ask the question: "Suppose I bring help?"

The grimace was on Shelton's face again. "You do that, banker. You do that." His eyes were on Abel's face. "I'll tell you what'll happen. The first time you try to get the kid out of a window or bring help or to kill me, she'll die and so will Missus Clark." He nodded toward the kitchen door. "All right, get some supper."

Jane crossed the dining room to the kitchen, Abel following. In spite of Shelton's warnings, Abel had a feeling that this was their only chance, even though it meant a gamble with Laurie's life. There must be another gun in the house. Neal had taken his revolver and rifle. Shelton had the .38. Then Abel remembered Neal saying there was a .22 in the pantry.

The instant Abel reached the kitchen, he shut the door. "Where's the Twenty-Two, Jane? Neal said you had one. I'll kill him. I've got to. We can't take any chances on waiting."

Jane's self-control broke. She dropped the grocery basket and meat and, grabbing Abel by the shoulders, shook him. "No, no, no!" She began to cry, and Abel took her into his arms and held her until the moment of hysteria passed. Presently she stepped back and dried her eyes. "I'm sorry, Henry." She swallowed. "You're brave to even think about it, but we can't gamble with

Laurie's life. It's what Shelton wants us to do. We can't risk it."

So she thought he was brave. Nobody else did. Nobody else had ever said it to him. Well, he'd show her that he was. He walked past her into the pantry. She didn't understand. If they waited, they'd die. In some terrible way that only Tuck Shelton would think of. Better take a gamble now than wait until it was too late.

He examined one shelf after another, but the gun wasn't in sight. He heard Jane crying from where she stood beside the kitchen table. He stepped back, wondering if he'd better get a chair and examine the top shelf that was above his head. If the gun was in the pantry, it must be up there on that shelf.

He raised a hand and felt along the shelf, knowing that if it was close to the edge, he'd find it and wouldn't have to get a chair. Then he felt it and drew it off the shelf. It was loaded. He swung around, then stopped dead still, the gun in his hand. Shelton was standing in the dining room doorway, his revolver lined on Jane, his gaze on Abel.

"Lay it on the table, banker," Shelton said.

Abel obeyed, his head starting to hammer again. Jane had been right when she'd said this was exactly what Shelton wanted them to do. He'd given them a minute or two, then he'd come into the kitchen and had caught Abel in the act of doing what Shelton had guessed he'd do.

Now, with the gun on the table, Shelton motioned Abel toward the back door. He said: "You're a God-damned fool, banker. I warned you, but no, you wouldn't listen." He backed toward the dining room door. "Go for help, mister. Run like hell. I'm going upstairs. By the time you get back, it'll be too late and you'll see something you'll wish. . . ."

"No, Shelton!" Jane cried. "No. He won't do anything again. I promise. We'll do exactly like you tell us to."

Shelton hesitated as if weighing her words against the promise he'd made. "I don't know, Missus Clark," he said. "I gave you my proposition, but this fool didn't want to take it."

"I promise!" Jane cried. "I promise."

Shelton seemed pleased. "I want your husband to be here before I do anything. All right, we'll see. Now go get that wood, banker. We'll find out if you've got enough sense to learn anything."

Shelton wheeled and returned to the parlor. Jane said: "Henry, are you going to do what I asked this time?"

He looked at her, utterly miserable. "I don't know. I thought I was right. What can we do?"

"Wait," she said. "We won't do anything until Neal gets back. It would be a poor bargain for him if he got here and killed Shelton, and then found out Laurie was dead."

"So we live with a crazy man," Abel said. "Stay here and wait on him and not know whether we'll be dead or alive the next minute. Is that what you want to do?"

"Yes," Jane said. "It's what we've got to do."

Abel didn't say anything more. He built a fire and walked slowly across the back porch and on to the woodshed. He sat down on the chopping block and rolled and lighted a cigarette. He thought of a dozen possibilities and realized that none would work, but he knew he was right and Jane was wrong. If Neal had to go on clear to the Barney Lakes with Rolfe and Doc Santee, he'd be gone for two or three days. Abel knew he could not stand it that long. Neither could Jane nor Laurie.

If he could think of anything that promised success, he'd do it no matter what Jane thought. He could carry a ladder that leaned against the woodshed around the side of the house and get Laurie out through the window. No, Shelton would hear him.

He looked around the woodshed. He saw a rusty knife on a shelf inside the door. He could slip that inside his shirt and use

152

it on Shelton when he was asleep. There was a hatchet lying in the chips in a corner. He could slip that under his belt and, when he had a chance, split Shelton's head open like a cabbage.

On and on, one idea after another running through his mind, and then the first returned and he went through the list again. They were like petitions to heaven on an Oriental prayer wheel. Everyone promised failure because Abel knew he wasn't man enough to try any of them with the slightest chance of success. If he were Neal, he could try and maybe succeed, but he wasn't Neal. He was Henry Abel, scared of his own wife.

He got up and began splitting wood with slow, methodical strokes, but his mind wasn't on his work. He kept thinking of Laurie, alone in her bed. She'd be waking up soon and Jane would have to go to her. So, sick with a baffling sense of futility, he told himself he would do nothing. Like Jane, he would wait.

CHAPTER NINETEEN

Neal realized he had made a mistake the instant he was in the open, with bullets kicking up geysers of dirt all around him. A slug sliced through his pants just above the knee and raised a painful welt along his thigh. Another cut through his left boot above his ankle. Then, halfway to the top, he dived headlong to one side, gaining the protection of a low ridge of rock.

He lay on his belly, sucking in great gulps of air. Both Joe Rolfe and Doc Santee had opened up from the other side of the road, Rolfe nearly to the top of the ridge, Santee about halfway up. Now the firing stopped.

The sun was almost down; the light was thinning rapidly. Neal wondered if that was the reason he was alive. Darley had been shooting against the setting sun. Perhaps the slanting rays had blinded him. Or he may have been worried by the burst of fire from Rolfe's and Santee's guns. Or he might be a bad shot who just couldn't do any better.

The minutes dragged by, with Neal hugging the downhill side of the rock. He was so close to where Darley had forted up that the promoter was bound to score a hit if Neal made a standing target. He couldn't raise his head to see exactly where Darley was hiding, or if there was a weakness in his position.

All Neal could do was to lie here with his nose in the dirt and curse himself for an impulsive action that had put him into this jam. He was not going to be of any help to either Jane or Laurie if he got himself killed out here on Horse Ridge. But that line of thinking did not bring him any comfort. He had to know about Shelton. He had got this far with nothing more than a scratch. Maybe he could go all the way next time.

One moment he'd been telling himself he was damned lucky to be alive and he'd been a fool, the next moment he knew he couldn't go on lying here. Fool or not, he had to do something. He tried to hold himself back, tried to assure himself that Rolfe and Santee were working around on the other side of Darley and they'd have the man boxed. Logic was one thing, but lying here and thinking about what might be happening to Jane and Laurie was another.

Carefully he wormed his way to the end of the ledge, and, pulling his gun, eared back the hammer. He eased his gun around the rock and threw a quick shot in Darley's general direction, then jerked his hand back.

Darley answered the shot immediately, his bullet kicking up dust a few inches from where Neal's hand had been. Rolfe and Santee cut loose again. Neal couldn't pinpoint their positions, but, judging from the sound of the firing, he was convinced they had not moved up.

Neal cursed, a closed fist pounding the dirt. They were stuck. One man had them pinned down. Neal called: "Throw out your rifle, Darley! I'm coming up after you."

"Come ahead," Darley said, "but I'm not throwing out my rifle."

Neal glanced at the sun. Time he was moving in. It would be dark soon, and Darley would make a break for it then. That was a chance Neal refused to take. If he lunged into the open again, he'd get it. Darley would expect him to show up from the side he'd just fired from. If he went the other way, he'd have a better chance, with Darley a poor shot and having slow reactions.

Slow reactions! Neal considered that a moment, thinking of the way the man had fought the day before in his office. He wasn't a driver. He'd landed one good punch, but he hadn't followed up.

This was the only angle he could think of, the best bet for escape from what was an untenable position. Quickly Neal slid his hand back to the end of the ledge, pulled himself up on one hand and his knees as high as he could without exposing the hump of his back, and fired.

He came upright like a jack-in-the-box, whirled, and dived toward another ledge farther up the hill and closer to the road. Darley fired as Neal had been sure he would, and fired again just as Neal gained his new position, the bullet striking a corner of the rock and screaming through space.

"Joe!" Neal called. "Can you hear me?"

"Yeah, I can hear you," Rolfe answered.

"Doc?"

"Over here," Santee answered. "I just picked up another ten feet. We've got him hipped."

"Hold on," Rolfe cut in. "No use getting shot up. I think the bastard's hit."

"I can't wait any longer!" Neal shouted. "I'm the closest. I'm going after him."

"We'll all move when you do," Santee said. "Can you see where he is?"

"No," Neal said, "but we've got him from three sides. One of us ought to be able to see him."

"He's down in a hole," Santee said. "Rocks all around him, but I don't have far to go before I can look down at him."

"Come ahead!" Darley screamed. "I'll get Clark, you Goddamned sons-of-. . . ."

Darley never finished his sentence. Rolfe came running in along the lip of the rim. Darley, his attention on Neal, didn't see him until he fired, and in that same instant Neal and Santee charged Darley's position, Neal angling slightly to the right and

Santee crossing the road and coming in from the opposite direction.

Rolfe had the longest way to come. He was zigzagging, bending low, shooting steadily as he ran. Darley fired at him, and that gave Neal the small advantage of time he needed. He was the closest. Before Darley could turn his gun on him, Neal took a long jump to the top of one of the rocks that hid Darley. He fired and missed, and Darley threw a shot just as Santee cut loose; the doctor's bullet raked Darley along the side. It was enough to throw him off.

Darley had the one chance at Neal and missed, but this time Neal didn't miss. He caught Darley in the chest, knocking him against the rock behind him. His feet slid out from under him and he sat down, his gun dropping from his hand.

"Got him!" Neal called.

He saw Fay Darley, lying on her back in the bottom of the hole, her hands and feet tied, a dark streak of dried blood on her forehead and down one side of her face.

"Cut me loose, Neal," Fay said. "He slugged me with a gun barrel and tied me up."

Neal holstered his gun and, jerking out his pocket knife, cut the ropes that held the woman.

Darley wasn't dead, but he was going fast. Neal whirled on him, demanding: "Where is Shelton?"

"Go to hell," Darley said.

Santee jumped down into the hole beside Neal and, squatting beside the wounded man, opened his shirt and shook his head. "You're finished, Darley. You better talk."

Darley, who had never been a brave man, died like one. He said again—"Go to hell."—and fell sideways, blood trickling down his chin.

Neal helped Fay to her feet. She leaned against a rock, her eyes shut. She put a hand to her forehead, muttering: "My

God, my head feels like he's still hitting me."

Rolfe holstered his gun and, climbing to the top of the rock, held down his hand to her. She opened her eyes, and took his hand. Neal gave her a boost out of the hole with Rolfe pulling on her hand, then she stood beside Rolfe, swaying uncertainly until Neal scrambled up beside her and put an arm around her. Rolfe slid off the other side of the rock and helped her down.

"What happened?" Neal said. "Where's Shelton?"

"In town." Fay's knees gave and she sat down, her back against the rock. "We've got the money. It's in the saddlebags." She motioned toward a clump of junipers where their horses were tied. "We were headed for the lakes. Shelton was going to meet us there. I didn't know why he stayed in town until after we left."

Neal glanced at Santee, who had climbed out of the hole and was watching, then at Rolfe, who was holding a wadded-up bandanna against a bullet gash in his left arm.

Rolfe said impatiently: "All right, tell us about it."

"Are you going to arrest me?" Fay asked.

"You're damned right," Rolfe said.

"On what charge?"

"I don't know, but I'll throw you into the cooler for something. Go on now, tell us what happened."

"I tried to help," she said. "I wanted you to catch us. I couldn't let Shelton go ahead with what he'd planned. After we left town, I saw Manion and I shot at him. He went after you, didn't he?"

"That's right," Rolfe said.

Fay Darley was not the woman Neal had seen in town that morning, or beside the river the day before. She was dirty, her hair disheveled, her face contorted with pain, but for the first time he sensed a quality in her that had been missing before. Compassion. Or mercy. He wasn't sure. Perhaps humility.

"Jud took you for Shelton," Neal said.

"I was riding Shelton's horse," she said. "That was why. He was a long ways off. I don't think Shelton intended to meet us at the lakes. He wanted us out of town, thinking Rolfe would chase us. This whole swindle was Shelton's idea in the beginning, but I don't think the money was what he wanted any of the time."

"What did he want?" Neal asked.

"Those notes," she went on as if she hadn't heard the question. "He wanted to hurt you. I thought they were a bluff. It's like I said yesterday. They were trying to get you out of town so they wouldn't have any trouble with Stacey. They even put Ruggles on you. He was supposed to wound you. That way you'd be home in bed. Shelton wanted you there so he could kill you. He's a crazy man, Neal. I knew it all the time. Or I should have. He's the only man I ever met who didn't care anything about me. I was like another man to him."

"Who is he?"

"I don't know," Fay said. "Darley met him in Arizona. Darley's always been a promoter of some kind. Or a con man working the mining camps. Shelton told him about this country . . . the lakes and the high desert . . . and convinced him he could make a fortune here. That's why he came. At least that's what Darley and I thought, but Shelton had something else in his head. I didn't know what it was, and I don't believe Darley did until the other day. He told me on the way out. I couldn't stand it. When we got here, we stopped to rest our horses. We were on the ground and I shot him in the leg. He slugged me and tied me up. He said he was going to fight it out. He said you men would kill him if you could, and he'd bled too much to make a hard ride."

"Fay,"—Neal knelt beside her—"what did he tell you?"

She looked at him, trying to smile. "Funny, isn't it?" she said in a low voice. "Most of the things I said to you weren't lies. I didn't think you'd believe them, but I knew they planned to kill you and I wanted to keep them from doing it." She looked up at Rolfe. "Will it help any? What I did? Darley might have gone clear to the lakes. You might have lost him."

"Sure, it'll help," Rolfe said.

Neal took her hands. "Fay, what did Darley tell you?"

She put her head against the rock and closed her eyes. "Shelton's nursing a grudge against you. He has been for eight years. He planned this to get revenge. Turn everybody against you. Hang you maybe. Injure your family. Anything to make you suffer. Even take it out on your little girl. When I heard that, I knew I had to stop Darley. I thought I could ride back and warn you, but he wasn't going to take any chances. . . ."

She opened her eyes. Neal was gone, running down the slope toward Redman.

Rolfe called: "Wait, Neal! You'll need help!"

Santee said: "Let him go, Joe. This is a job he'll want to do himself."

CHAPTER TWENTY

As Neal ran down the slope to his horse, he remembered how it had been that time, stepping out of Olly Earl's hardware store and shooting the Shelly gang to pieces, with only Ed Shelly escaping. But Tuck Shelton could not be Ed Shelly. Joe Rolfe had proved that to Neal's satisfaction. Now Fay said Shelton had nursed a grudge against him for eight years, so Shelton must, in some way, be tied up with the Shelly outfit.

Neal swung into the saddle and cracked steel to Redman. Fay said Shelton was a crazy man. She was right. No one but a crazy man would want to injure Laurie. Neal had told himself that repeatedly from the moment he'd received the second note saying Neal's wife and girl would pay for the murder of Ed Shelly's father and brother.

Only Henry Abel stood between Laurie and Shelton. He would be no match for a maniac. Then Neal realized he had spurred Redman until the horse was in a hard run. He pulled the gelding down to a slower pace. If he killed the animal between here and town, he'd be on foot, at least until Rolfe and Santee caught up with him, and they would be slowed by having to take care of a sick woman and leading a horse with a dead man tied across the saddle.

Dusk settled down, then darkness, the last scarlet trace of the sunset dying above the Cascades. To Neal Clark, with this driving sense of urgency in him, the town seemed as far away as ever. As he rode, the fear grew in him that no matter how long

161

it took him or what he did, he would be too late.

Neal nearly killed Redman that night. He would rein the horse down, then, before he realized it, he'd have him running again. During the long ride to town, he was vaguely aware of the beat of hoofs against the sandy soil of the road, of the slack shapes of the junipers as they flashed by, of the stars overhead, of the wind rushing down from the high peaks of the Cascades that penetrated into the vary marrow of his bones.

He was aware of these things, but they did not form a conscious pattern. Only time mattered. Redman's life was not important as long as the horse stayed on his feet long enough to get to town. Neal's own life was nothing unless he could barter it for Laurie's. And Jane's. But he had no idea how he could manage it. He couldn't even guess what he would find when he got home.

So he rode, the hours and miles falling behind, and hope that had been in him when he'd left Horse Ridge began to fade until it was no hope at all. When at last he reined his lathered, heaving horse to a stop in front of his house, he saw that there were lights in Laurie's room and in the parlor.

Cold logic told Neal that a sensible man would have done whatever he intended to do and been on his way hours ago, but now he saw the lights and hope blazed high in him again. There would be no light in Laurie's room unless she was all right, he thought.

Neal dismounted and crossed the yard to the porch, moving as silently as he could. He turned the knob, opened the front door, and stepped inside. Closing the door, he drew his gun and eased along the hall to the parlor, the floor squeaking under his feet. He had forgotten about the squeaky boards.

He should have gone around to the back. Too late. The parlor door was open and light fell through it into the hall; he could not go past the door without being seen, if Shelton was in the parlor. But Shelton might be anywhere in the house, even up in Laurie's room with a gun pointed at her head.

So Neal waited, hearing no sound except the ticking of the clock on the mantel, waited while sweat dripped down his face. After his wild ride, plagued by a thousand fears, impelled by his compulsive urge to find out what had happened, he was caught here in his hall.

Then he heard Shelton's even-toned, monotonous voice: "Come in, Mister Clark, with your hands up, unless you want your banker killed."

For a moment Neal couldn't move. This was not what he had expected. Shelton was in the parlor, so he must have known Neal was in the house and he had let him stand there, finding pleasure in the torment of uncertainty that he knew was plaguing Neal. The paralysis passed. He had no way of knowing whether Henry Abel was under the man's gun or not, but he couldn't take any chances. He slipped the gun under his waistband and walked through the door, his hands high.

Abel sat on the couch, his hands folded on his lap, and in the lamplight his face was shiny with beads of sweat. Shelton stood in the fringe of light, his gun lined on Abel. He did not indicate by even a slight movement of his head that he had seen Neal come in.

"That's fine, Mister Clark," Shelton said, emphasizing the mister. "I expected obedience from an intelligent man like you. Now lay your gun on the table. Draw up a chair and sit down. If you try to shoot me, I'll kill you and your banker, and everyone else in the house."

"Laurie?" Neal asked.

"She's all right," Abel said.

"So far," Shelton added significantly. "She's in her room. Her mother's with her. As a matter of fact, Mister Clark, we've had a real good evening. I was sorry to hear you ride up."

So he'd known the instant Neal had dismounted in front of the house. It wouldn't have made any difference if he had come in through the back door. Probably it was locked anyhow. He hesitated, wondering if he had any chance to get his gun into action before Shelton killed him. A slim one, he thought, but it meant throwing Abel's life away, and he couldn't do that. Not yet, so he obeyed Shelton's orders, slowly drawing his gun from holster and laying it on the table. Then he sat down.

"I rode my horse harder than I should have," Neal said. "I'd like for Henry to go out and take care of him."

"A cowman first, a banker second," Shelton said. "All right, Abel, you do that. Rub the horse down. He's a good animal. We've got to take care of him. I'll need him before morning."

Slowly Shelton turned so his gun covered Neal. Abel rose, glancing at Neal as if trying to read his mind. Here was their chance, Neal thought, and Abel would take advantage of it. He could move the ladder that leaned against the back of the house and put it to Laurie's window. They could escape, Laurie and Jane. Neal was a hostage, but that didn't make any difference. He was a dead man anyway.

Neal nodded and Abel started toward the dining room. He reached it just as Shelton said: "Go out through the front door, banker, and lead the horse around the house. Leave the back door locked."

Shelton was silent until Abel reached the hall door, then he laughed. It was the first time, Neal thought, that he had ever heard the man laugh, an odd sound that broke out of him suddenly and was gone as quickly as it came, leaving no lingering trace of humor on the man's cruel mouth.

"You're a pair of fools, Clark," Shelton said. "I know what you're thinking. He'll ride that horse downtown and get help. Or find a gun. Or get back into the house through a window and surprise me. All right, banker, you try it. If you do, there's a woman and a kid upstairs who'll die, but, if you do what I tell you, they won't get hurt." He nodded at Neal. "This is the bastard I want, not the woman or the kid or you, banker. Savvy that?"

"I savvy," Abel said.

"I'll give you fifteen minutes," Shelton said. "You'd better be damned sure you're back here by that time."

Abel left the room. When the door closed, Shelton said: "I reckon you caught up with Darley and his woman."

"On Horse Ridge," Neal said. "Darley's dead."

"Shoot himself?" Shelton asked.

"No," Neal said, and told him what had happened.

Shelton shrugged. "Darley was the kind of man I needed in most ways, but he lacked guts. I'm surprised he forted up that way. He wouldn't have if she hadn't shot him and he figured you'd never fetch him back alive." Shelton turned his head and spit in contempt at the fireplace. "Women! What damned good are they? It was Darley's idea fetching her here. Now she shoots him 'cause she's worried about you and your kid. I figured she was too smart to do a trick like that."

"Maybe she's human," Neal said.

"Meaning I'm not? You're right, but you made me what I am. You're to blame, Clark. If your wife and kid get hurt, you're to blame. For eight years I haven't wanted to do anything but squeeze the hell out of your soul. I have, haven't I?"

"You know you have," Neal said.

Shelton sat down, the gun dangling between his legs. "This is just a beginning. Now you're gonna know why. That's important, Clark. I've lived tonight a million times in my mind, dreaming about how I'd be sitting here just like I am now and telling you what you done eight years ago. Listen to me, Clark. Listen damned good because you haven't got long to listen to anything. If you're thinking of that Twenty-Two in the pantry, you can quit. Or your Thirty-Eight that Abel had. I've got both of 'em."

Shelton was sitting so he could watch the stairs and Neal, but the hall at the head of the stairs was dark. Neal had been hoping Jane would get the .38 and shoot at Shelton. She wasn't a very good shot, but it would give Neal a chance to try for his gun on the table. Now even that slender thread of hope was broken.

"I'm listening," Neal said.

"You've been wondering if Ed Shelly was around here, haven't you?" Shelton asked. "And you've wondered what I had to do with him. You and Rolfe scratched around trying to figure it out . . . the notes and Ruggles being here and who I was. The name Shelton's purty close to Shelly, ain't it?"

Neal nodded. "I'm still listening."

"Well, when you shot the Shelly outfit, you made the biggest mistake a man ever made. My name is Tuck Shelly. When I came here, I called myself Shelton because it was close enough to Shelly to make you wonder, but you couldn't prove nothing. I took the shot at you last night and missed on purpose. I hired Ruggles to come here and shoot you. Not bad. Just enough to lay you up so you'd be here when I wanted you. I missed on that. Ruggles wasn't as good with his gun as he was supposed to be."

Neal sat with his hands fisted on his lap, knowing Shelton was purposely stringing this out to make him suffer, but not knowing how long he could stand it. "All right, all right," he said. "Let's have the story." Funny, now that he thought back. Neither he nor Rolfe had seen the real significance in the names Shelly and Shelton.

"I've dreamed about this for eight years," Shelton said. "I don't aim to hurry now. I've got to make a few hours do to you what all them years done to me. I'm Ed Shelly's uncle. I was out there in the desert with my brother and his two boys. I was supposed to help on the hold-up, and, if I had, you wouldn't be alive today, but, just before they hit the bank, I sprained my ankle, so Ed took my place."

He waggled a forefinger at Neal, his voice suddenly becoming high and shrill. "I didn't have any kids of my own. I guess I never loved anybody in my life except Ed Shelly. He looked like me and acted like me. When he was little, I took care of him a hell of a lot more'n his dad ever done. Ed's mother died when he was a baby.

"He was just a kid when you killed him. He had no business coming to town, but they had to have someone to hold the horses. You hit him. By the time he got to camp, he'd bled bad. I helped him off his horse and watched him die. From your bullet, Clark."

He got up and walked to Neal. He slapped him with his left hand, the gun gripped in his right, then struck him on the other side of the face, rocking Neal's head. He backed off, saliva running down his chin from his lips. He wiped a shirt sleeve across his mouth, and began to curse.

"I can't hurt you enough, Clark. Not half enough. I watched him die and I couldn't even go for a doctor. I couldn't do anything but watch him die, I tell you. He did, and I buried him. I sent that note from Salt Lake City so you'd know that sooner or later you'd get it. I spent my time since then thinking about what I'd do to you and who I'd get to help me. Darley was the best I could find.

"Ever since I came here I've watched you. You lost your friends. We seen to that. I thought they'd hang you. They came purty close to stringing you up, too, but they didn't, so I figured this was the next best. Get Rolfe chasing after Darley who had the money. Manion seeing 'em and telling Rolfe was luck. I hadn't counted on that, but I figured somebody would come up and see the safe was cleaned out, and guess that Darley had the money."

Neal didn't move, his hands clutched so tightly the knuckles were white. As he watched Shelton, he saw spit run down the man's chin again. His eyes were wide and wild, and Neal knew that there was nothing he could say or do that would touch him.

"Get up!" Shelton shouted. "By God, you're gonna get on your feet and go upstairs with me. You'll watch what I'm gonna do to your wife and kid."

"It's me you want," Neal reminded him. "You said it wasn't Jane or Laurie."

Again Shelton wiped his mouth with his sleeve. "Did I say that?" He laughed just as he had before, a laugh that was no real laugh at all. "What are words? Nothing, Clark. Nothing! Now get on your feet and start up them stairs."

CHAPTER TWENTY-ONE

Neal rose, knowing that Shelton had only one purpose, to torture him in every way he could. That had been his purpose in sending the threatening notes about Jane and Laurie; it was his reason for making them suffer now.

"I'm not going," Neal said. "Go ahead and shoot me. That's what you want to do, isn't it?"

"No!" Shelton shouted angrily. "I want to twist your guts around your heart till you're dead. I won't tell you again. Get up them stairs."

"I won't go," Neal said.

This was something Shelton could not comprehend. He stood motionlessly, breathing hard. He cocked his gun, aiming it at Neal's chest, then he lowered it and shook his head. "I ain't letting you off that easy. We'll wait till your banker gets back."

Shelton motioned for Neal to sit down again. For a time he eyed Neal, then he began to pace around the room. Watching him, Neal thought he understood. Shelton had spent eight years planning this, relishing in anticipation his revenge upon the man he hated. Now, having reached the end of the game, he didn't know how to extract the greatest pleasure from his vengeance. Anticipation, Neal knew, gave more satisfaction than realization, and in that regard Shelton was perfectly normal.

Neal's gun was still on the table where he had placed it when he'd first come into the room, not more than ten feet from where he sat. He could make a dive for it, maybe reach the table, then Shelton would cut him down. Probably not kill him. Maybe shoot him in the leg and let him bleed to death. It was a price Neal would pay if he could save Jane and Laurie, but what possible good would it do?

No, Neal had to wait until he saw at least a slim chance of success. Henry Abel was outside. Suddenly Neal remembered the gun he had taken from Ruggles and tossed into a manger in the barn. But Abel wouldn't know about it. If Neal had thought to tell him . . . had given him some kind of signal before he left the house. . . .

No good, Neal told himself. Henry Abel was not a man to get a gun and come back into the house and shoot Tuck Shelton. He wasn't a man to run, either. He had too much loyalty for that. But for the moment he was outside and he might think of something. So Neal sat there, sweat pouring down his face, his belly muscles as tight as a drum.

Shelton sat down, leaning forward a little, his gun still in his right hand. He remained motionless for several minutes, the clock on the mantel ticking off the seconds with slow monotony. The man's eyes were riveted on him, but Neal wondered if Shelton was actually seeing him. A strange expression had taken the place of the wolfish eagerness on Shelton's face. It seemed to Neal that Shelton was so lost in the past that the present had ceased to exist for him.

Neal thought he had a chance now. He rose slowly, for a moment thinking that Shelton was in a sort of self-imposed hypnotic trance. But it was only wishful thinking. Shelton motioned with the gun, and Neal dropped back.

"Sit down, Clark," Shelton said. "I ain't ready to kill you yet, but I will if you make me. I was thinking how it's been with you . . . a big ranch and a bank. A purty wife and a kid you love and a fine house . . . everything I didn't have."

He licked his lips, and leaned forward again in his chair. He began to talk fast, as if words could relieve the pent-up hatred that had festered in him so many years.

"My brother Buck never thought much of me. I was a bad one by his lights. I was younger'n he was, and smarter. He didn't know anything except to take what he wanted by force. His wife died when Ed was little. That's why I raised him. Buck was so damned ornery he wouldn't take care of his own kid, so Ed didn't like him, but he did like me.

"I tried to keep Ed from ever riding the Owlhoot. We kept him straight for a long time. Had him in school in Eugene. He didn't even know what we were till he was about thirteen. Finally Buck said he was gonna make a man out of him or kill him trying. That's what he done, with your bullet. I don't care anything about you killing Buck. Or the other boy. They had it coming. Sooner or later I'd have done it if you hadn't, but you made a mistake when you shot Ed."

Shelton got up and, walking to the table, picked up Neal's gun and slipped it under his waistband, then came back and sat down. Neal didn't understand why Shelton felt this need to talk, to explain to the man he was determined to kill, but he did realize something he hadn't before. Much of Shelton's brooding hatred had been fastened upon his brother, but Buck Shelly was dead, so he could not take his revenge on him. Only Neal.

"I told you Ed was a lot like me," Shelton went on. "I loved him. I never loved nobody else before or afterwards. I told you I watched him die, by inches, out there in a dirty dry camp in the desert, and I couldn't do a damned thing. I couldn't move him. I couldn't leave him to go after a doctor. I didn't have any decent grub for him. When he died, I died, too. You killed him. When you done that, you killed me, but you didn't kill me dead. That was another mistake. You should have put a bullet into me."

The front door opened and closed. Abel was coming back.

For a moment a wild hope was in Neal that Abel might have found Ruggles's gun, that he'd come out of the hall with the gun blazing. Even if Abel died, Neal would have a chance to rush Shelton. That was all he could do, with his own gun now under Shelton's waistband.

But he knew at once he was like any drowning man reaching for a straw. Abel appeared in the doorway, pale and shivering from the cold or from fear. He said: "You rode that horse pretty hard, Neal, but I rubbed him down and I think he'll be all right."

Shelton was on his feet, his gun on Neal. He motioned for Abel to sit down. When Abel had obeyed, Shelton said: "Now, Mister Clark, we'll go upstairs. Ed was like my own son to me, so I'm going to kill your girl. I've got to, you see, to be fair."

Neal leaned back, hands gripping the arms of his chair. He said: "You'll have to kill me here, Shelton. I told you I wouldn't do it."

"I think you will. If you don't, your banker gets it. First in the knees. Then both elbows. I won't kill him. He'll live, but he won't be worth a damn for anything. How about it?"

Neal looked at Abel, knowing he would have to do what Shelton wanted. He might have a chance while they were going up the stairs, or after they reached the hall. But he couldn't sit here and see Henry Abel shot to pieces, and Shelton knew he couldn't.

"Tell him to go to hell, Neal," Abel said. "He won't touch Laurie if he can't get you up there to watch it."

Shelton whirled on Abel, cursing him. Neal, looking at Abel, felt a rush of admiration for the little man who had called himself a coward, who had many times admitted he was thoroughly cowed by his wife, and who must have been through hell during these hours since Shelton had been in the house. Yet he had made this gesture, and Neal sensed he was right. Shelton probably wouldn't harm Laurie unless Neal was there to watch.

"Wait, Shelton," Neal said. "You need some advice."

Shelton turned his gaze on Neal, his eyes wild again. He said: "By God, I don't need any advice from you."

"Will you listen to me?" When Shelton was silent, Neal rushed on. "Darley had the money. If he'd got away, he'd have waited somewhere for you, wouldn't he? You'd have split and then gone on, after you finished with me. That right?"

Diverted for the moment, Shelton nodded. Neal hurried on: "This way, with Darley dead, and Santee and the sheriff bringing the money in, you'll leave here broke. Well, it just occurred to me that you're stupid to ride out that way as long as the bank's safe is filled with cash."

Again Henry Abel did a surprising thing. He laughed, a good, deep laugh as if he actually saw some humor in this situation. He said: "Shelton, that would sure put the frosting on the cake for you, leaving here with your pockets full of Neal's money. He'd die knowing you were going to have it easy the rest of your life and he was paying for it."

"That would be smart, wouldn't it?" Shelton snarled. "Me walking down through town just as old man Rolfe showed up. Or some of these town bastards seeing me go into the bank with you."

"Rolfe and Santee won't be back till sunup," Neal said. "They've got Fay who won't be able to ride fast, and they're fetching in a dead man to boot. As for the town bastards, I guess you've fixed it so they wouldn't believe anything good of me. If they caught us cleaning out the bank safe, they'd think it was my doing."

"They sure would," Abel said. "They'd hang you and pat Shelton on the back probably figuring he was trying to protect the bank's money."

This plainly appealed to Shelton. He scratched an ear thoughtfully, looking at Neal and then Abel, and Neal again. It wasn't the money so much, Neal thought, but rather the fact that his revenge would be lengthened and sweetened. He didn't want this to end or he'd have finished it before now. He was like a child with a piece of hard candy in his mouth, sucking it, trying to make it last as long as he could.

"Got another horse in the barn?" Shelton asked finally.

"Jane's mare," Neal answered. "She's a good animal."

"A side-saddle?"

"Jane rides one, but there's another saddle in the barn we can use."

"How come you're giving me advice?" Shelton asked. "Pretty good advice, too, seems to me."

"If you kill me now, it's over with," Neal said, "but if we clean the bank safe out and start across the desert, I'll get you. I don't know how, but I'll find a way."

Shelton shook his head, a tight smile on his lips. "A man in your shape naturally looks for a miracle. You won't find it, Clark. I've lived this too many times. I won't let anything happen. The fact is, I'm way ahead of you. Now I'll tell you what we will do."

Shelton paused, letting the seconds ribbon out. For a little while hope had been high in Neal. Once he got Shelton into the barn, he'd do something. He'd get hold of Ruggles's gun. Or a pitchfork. Throw the lantern into Shelton's face. Anything, he thought wildly. At least he'd have Shelton out of the house and Jane might escape with Laurie through the front door. But now, seeing the satisfaction in Shelton's face, he felt the hope die.

"We'll go out to the barn and saddle the horses," Shelton said. "Then we'll go to the bank and you'll open the safe. We'll take the money and be out of town before sunup. I hid my tracks once from Joe Rolfe and I can do it again." He nodded at Abel. "While Clark's saddling up, you have Missus Clark dress the kid. She's going with us. I'll give you five minutes to get her to the barn. It'll take Clark that long to saddle the horses. I'm toting the kid. If anything goes wrong, she gets it. Understand, both of you?"

Abel nodded. Neal stood up, thinking dully that he should have foreseen this. Shelton had known all along that the best way to hurt Neal was through Laurie. Whatever Neal did, he must do it before Abel reached the barn with Laurie. After that he would be helpless.

"Funny I didn't think of this before," Shelton said. "There's been a lot of talk about the Barney Mountain lakes. Well, that's where we're going. I'm going to throw your kid into one of them lakes, Clark, and you're going to watch."

Neal didn't look at Abel as he walked toward the dining room. He couldn't. He couldn't even think, but he knew Shelton would do exactly what he had threatened. If Abel had sense enough to take Laurie and make a run for it through the front door. . . .

"Wait, Clark," Shelton said. "Where's the key to the front door?"

"It's in the lock," Abel said. "I locked it when I came in."

"Maybe you're lying," Shelton said. "Don't make any difference, I guess. If you try taking the kid through that door, or through a window, I'll kill Clark. Understand? You've got five minutes. No more. All right, Clark. Find a lantern and light it. Let's get started."

Chapter Twenty-Two

Neal walked through the dining room into the kitchen, Shelton calling back to Abel: "Damn it, get that kid dressed! Five minutes. No more. Can't you get that through your head?"

Then Shelton was only a few feet behind Neal, with the cocked gun lined on his back. He said: "There's a lantern on the back porch."

"Light it," Shelton said.

Neal unlocked the back door and opened it. "Too much wind to keep a match going," he said.

"Then get it inside," Shelton snapped. "You trying to use your five minutes up before we even get to the barn?"

He was jumpy now and nervous. It was in his voice, and, when Neal took the lantern off the nail beside the door and stepped back into the kitchen, he saw it in Shelton's face. Once more hope flared up in Neal. A jumpy man makes mistakes. Up until now Shelton had been supremely confident, as if he was positive in his mind that he had the situation under control.

Neal jacked up the chimney, lit the lantern, and lowered the chimney. He went out through the back door, carrying the lantern; Shelton followed closely. They crossed the yard to the barn, and Neal could hear Shelton's hard breathing behind him.

He wondered about the nervousness in the man, and what had brought it on. Perhaps the desire for money had taken hold of him. No, that wasn't it. He had been motivated by revenge, not money, and it was unlikely he would change now. It must be that he was afraid Jane and Henry Abel would sacrifice Neal for Laurie and that would take the real flavor from his vengeance. His perverted mind had brooded so long upon the loss of his nephew that he had to have Laurie's life to satisfy him.

Neal opened the barn door as Shelton said: "Put the lantern down. I'll hold it. Get those saddles on."

Very deliberately Neal placed the lantern on the straw-littered floor of the barn. He said: "You'll never see Laurie, Shelton. Abel will tell Jane what your plan is and they'll take Laurie out through the front and get help."

"There won't be any help for you if they do," Shelton said. "Anyhow, your wife won't do that. She loves you, and, when a woman loves a man, she never thinks straight. She'll try to save both of you and that means she'll lose both of you."

Neal saddled Redman while Shelton stood directly back of the stall. Neal said: "This horse won't go very far tonight. I rode him too hard getting to town."

"Then you'll be walking," Shelton said. "I'll take the mare."

Neal stepped out of the stall, certain that more than five minutes had elapsed, but Shelton wasn't checking his watch. He'd wait until Laurie got there, Neal thought. But with Laurie in the barn, and Shelton as jumpy as he was. . . . Neal knew he couldn't wait; he couldn't risk it. Neal glanced at the wall with its clutter of bridles and halters and harness. He said: "What the hell did I do with his bridle?"

"You've got a dozen of 'em hanging in front of your nose," Shelton said angrily. "You're stalling, Clark, and I'm out of patience. To hell with the money. We're leaving town as soon as Abel gets here with the kid."

Neal was not surprised at that. The money in the bank had been only a temporary temptation to Shelton, but now fear had worked into him, the fear of failure, of not getting the revenge he had brooded on for so long. Rather than risk having anything go wrong during the time they were getting the money, Shelton would head for the desert and put as many miles between him and town as possible before sunup.

"I remember," Neal said, and walked back along the runway. "I tossed that bridle over here."

"Damn it, you want me to plug you now?" Shelton raged. "What's the matter with these bridles?"

Neal stopped back of the empty stall. "Most of them were brought in from the ranch when Dad was alive. I don't need them any more because I just keep two horses in town. I'm going to get Redman's bridle, so hold on a minute."

The kitchen screen slammed shut. Abel was coming with Laurie. Neal started toward the manger where he had dropped Ruggles's gun. This was the first time in his life he had ever been called upon to do a job of acting, and he wasn't sure he had put it across. Shelton, holding the lantern in one hand and the gun in the other, was looking at him one instant, then at the door to see if Abel and Laurie were in sight.

Neal reached the manger and leaned forward, right hand feeling for the gun. In that moment he had no doubt he was a dead man. Shelton, as jittery as he was now, would shoot the instant he saw the gun in Neal's hand.

For some strange reason Neal wasn't scared. He felt perfectly calm for the first time since he'd walked into the parlor tonight. He'd die with Shelton's bullet in him, but he had to live long enough to get Shelton. He could turn so his body would hide the gun.

"Hurry up!" Shelton shouted. "They're coming and you've only got one horse saddled."

"What's the hurry?" Neal asked, his hand running through the hay in the bottom of the manger. "I guess I'm not going anywhere without you."

"You're damned right you're not," Shelton snapped.

There was hay in the manager. Neal couldn't find the gun. He knew this was the right manger. Or was it? Had he tossed it . . . ?

Outside, Laurie called: "Daddy, are you there?"

"Come in here, Abel!" Shelton shouted. "It took you long enough to get here."

The sickness of final failure was in Neal. This was his only chance and Laurie was just outside. Then he found it. The gun had slipped down into the corner, Neal's searching fingers having missed it as they had stirred the hay.

He had the gun by the butt, saying—"I've got it, Shelton."— and cocked the gun and whirled. Shelton must have heard the sound of the hammer being pulled back. He must have seen the gun, too, but when he fired, it wasn't at Neal. He threw his shot at the door. He was trying to kill Laurie!

Neal's shot slammed into the echoes of Shelton's, the blasts ear-shattering inside the confines of the barn. Shelton was knocked back against the wall, falling into a tangle of harness. He tried to swing his gun to Neal. Neal shot him again. When Shelton's finger pulled the trigger, it was a paroxysm of death, the bullet kicking up a geyser of barn litter. His legs gave under him, and he sat down, his back against the barn wall, his mouth springing open as blood began to drool from the corners.

Shelton was dead. Neal didn't even stop to look at him. He threw the gun down and ran outside.

Jane was crossing the yard, crying: "Neal, Neal, are you all right?"

"Yes, I'm all right!" he called.

Henry Abel was on the ground. Laurie was huddled against the wall, crying. A bundle of bedclothes had fallen from Abel's hands. Neal gathered the child into his arms, not knowing what had happened or whether Abel was hard hit. Now his mind was numb from relief. It was as if he could not think beyond two facts that blotted out everything else in his mind. Shelton was dead and Laurie was still alive.

Jane knelt beside Abel. She said: "He's been hit. Carry him into the house. I'll get the lantern. You're all right, Laurie. You can walk."

Jane got the lantern, saying nothing about Shelton. She didn't faint from the sight of a man who had just been shot. She didn't even cry out. She was made of solid stuff, Neal thought, as he slipped a hand under Abel's neck and the other under his knees and lifted him from the ground.

They crossed the yard to the house, leaving terror behind them. Jane led the way with the lantern in one hand, and holding Laurie's little hand in her other one. Neal followed with Abel in his arms. Laurie was sniffling as she padded along in her bare feet. It would be a long time before she recovered entirely from the shock of this, but she would eventually, and she was alive, and for that Neal would be thankful as long as he lived.

Neal put Abel down on the couch in the parlor. "I'm not hurt," Abel said. "Just shock, I guess. Thought I was hit worse than I am."

Neal opened Abel's shirt and undershirt. It was only a flesh wound, and except for the soreness, it would give him little trouble. "Better put a bandage on it," Neal told Jane. "Just something to cover it until Doc gets a chance at it."

Neal picked Laurie up and held her. He leaned back in his chair, eyes closed, Laurie cuddling against him. He felt tired, so tired he couldn't move, but there was a sense of satisfaction in him. There would be no more nightmares for him. He could go back to the Circle C. He'd let Henry Abel run the bank, maybe coming in once a week to talk things over with him. He thought briefly that it wasn't what his father had wanted, but he immediately put it out of his mind. It didn't seem important.

He'd see Stacey in the morning. There was so much to be done here, things that took capital. If Stacey had money to invest, this was the right place for him. Suddenly he remembered the bundle of bedclothes Abel had dropped and his eyes snapped open. Jane was still kneeling at the couch.

"What kind of sandy were you pulling, Henry?" Neal asked. "That bundle. . . ."

"It was Henry's way of repaying you for what you'd done for him," Jane said. "That was what he told me. I couldn't argue with him. There wasn't time."

"Hell, I never did anything for you to repay me for," Neal said.

"You're wrong, Neal," Abel said. "I've never had any illusions about myself. I've been afraid of almost everything since the day I was shot, but you kept me in the bank. I guess I just had to prove I was some good to somebody. I knew Shelton would think that bundle was Laurie all wrapped up. I had her keep out of the light so she wouldn't get hurt and told her to call to you so Shelton would know she was there."

"I don't get it," Neal said. "What were you figuring on doing?"

"I didn't know for sure myself," Abel said. "I didn't know you had a gun out there, but I knew you were going to jump him, so I thought I'd hand the bundle to him and say this was Laurie. He'd be so mad he'd go crazy and you'd have your chance, but I didn't think of him shooting at me when I came in."

Neal was silent, thinking about how Shelton hadn't cared about his own life, or Neal's, really, but he knew that, if he killed Laurie and let Neal live, it would be a living death. Brutal, ruthless, maybe half mad, but he had understood perfectly how

Neal felt about Laurie. Unconsciously his arms tightened around her.

Jane came to him and knelt beside him. She said: "For a long time tonight I thought I'd lose you."

"I wondered myself," he said, and put an arm around her. He looked at Abel, shocked by the thought that here was a man he had known for a long time, and yet he had not understood him at all. Tonight Henry Abel had been willing to give up his life. He blurted: "Henry, you've got more guts than any man I know. I'm going to turn the bank over to you. We're moving out to the Circle C."

"I'd . . . I'd like that," Abel said simply.

Laurie had gone to sleep in Neal's arms. Jane was smiling at him, trying to hold back the tears that threatened to run over. He was lucky, luckier than he had ever realized. There was time to work on Sam Clark's big dreams. Time to help Jud Manion out and repay an old debt. Time to let O'Hara and Olly Earl and the rest of them know he didn't hate them. Why, there was time to live, now that the shadow of Ed Shelly was no longer upon him.

ABOUT THE AUTHOR

Wayne D. Overholser won three Spur Awards from the Western Writers of America and has a long list of fine Western titles to his credit. He was born in Pomeroy, Washington, and attended the University of Montana, University of Oregon, and the University of Southern California before becoming a public schoolteacher and principal in various Oregon communities. He began writing for Western pulp magazines in 1936 and within a couple of years was a regular contributor to Street & Smith's *Western Story Magazine* and Fiction House's *Lariat Story Magazine*. *Buckaroo's Code* (1947) was his first Western novel and remains one of his best. In the 1950s and 1960s, having retired from academic work to concentrate on writing, he would publish as many as four books a year under his own name or a pseudonym, most prominently as Joseph Wayne. *The Violent Land* (1954), *The Lone Deputy* (1957), *The Bitter Night* (1961), and *Riders of the Sundowns* (1997) are among the finest of the Overholser titles. *The Sweet and Bitter Land* (1950), *Bunch Grass* (1955), and *Land of Promises* (1962) are among the best Joseph Wayne titles, and Law Man (1953) is a most rewarding novel under the Lee Leighton pseudonym. Overholser's Western novels, whatever the byline, are based on a solid knowledge of the history and customs of the 19th-Century West, particularly when set in his two favorite Western states, Oregon and Colorado. Many of his novels are first-person narratives, a technique that tends to bring an added dimension of vividness to the frontier experiences of his narrators and frequently, as in *Cast a Long Shadow* (1957), the female characters one encounters are among the most memorable. He wrote his numerous novels with a consistent skill and an uncommon sensitivity to the depths of human character. Almost invariably, his stories weave a spell of their own with their scenes and images of social and economic forces often in conflict and the diverse ways of life and personalities that made the American Western frontier so unique a time and place in human history. *Death of a Cattle King* will be his next Five Star Western.